Ride

COMPETING FOR THE CUP

COMPETING FOR THE CUP

Bobbi JG Weiss

CANDLEWICK
ENTERTAINMENT

Chapter 1

NIGHT TERROR

In the stable, Kit wrapped her arms around TK.

The big black gelding's neck curved gracefully over her shoulder, his chin bumping against her back. Kit laughed as he raised and lowered his head over and over so that he could repeatedly chin-bump her, whuffling with contentment. His hot horse breath in contrast with the air made her realize she was freezing. Too excited to sleep after the excitement of the bonfire, she had sneaked out of bed and slipped on her mackintosh with just her jammies underneath. Her muck boots, while usually warm enough, weren't doing the job so well at the moment. She'd neglected to put on socks.

"Okay, big guy, I think the lovefest is over," she said. "I can't feel my toes."

Those were the last calm words she said. The next sounds out of her mouth were a series of incoherent wails as something right outside the stall made a sharp crashing noise, like a door slapping open in the wind. A ceiling timber fell, the heavy wood clattering against the wall, and Kit thought, *The roof is collapsing!*

TK squealed and jerked away from her, his nostrils flared. He pawed at the straw, his ears nervously swiveling back and forth, his eyes wide and darting. Kit's first instinct was to calm him, but for once she listened to her father's voice in her head: "A spooked horse is not a rational animal." So she shuffled backward and reached around to unlatch the stall door without taking her eyes off him.

The door wouldn't open. A timber had fallen right through the wooden railings, effectively locking it.

"Kit!"

The lights flickered on, and Kit's father, Rudy, appeared. He had pulled on a pair of work jeans and boots, but his coat wasn't entirely zipped up. He pulled at the timber stuck in the stall door, freeing it from the railings and hefting it to one side. "Out!" he commanded, sliding the stall door open.

Kit ran out as TK reared, terrified as the sounds of more falling timbers and the other horses' growing panic echoed around them.

"Go outside!" Rudy told her. "I'll take care of this!"

"No!" Kit shouted. "I'm not leaving you!" She almost screamed when hands grabbed her arms.

It was Will Palmerston. He must have heard the horses and come running at top speed from nearby Juniper Cottage. He worked as a stable hand, and his natural way with horses was quite amazing. He took one look at the wreckage in the corridor and said, "It's not safe in here—you need to get out!"

"No, I need to help Dad and TK!"

Will leaned down, staring directly into her eyes. "Kit. Go."

Kit resisted. Timbers, old equipment, and bales of hay were still dropping from the ceiling, and she wasn't about to leave her loved ones in danger.

"Hey," Will said, his voice softer but no less commanding. "Trust me."

Will's steady blue eyes met her own, and in that moment, Kit trusted him. And she wasn't sure she could be of any help inside the barn, either. She let go of his arms and ran outside.

She stood in the courtyard, covering her face and trying to figure out what she should do. Just as she decided to ignore all good sense and barrel back into the chaos, her roommate, Anya Patel, and several other students from nearby houses came running up, all of them holding robes and coats closed against the frigid England night. "Are you all right?" Anya panted, her words barely audible amid the mayhem of horses whinnying and people shouting.

"No! TK is freaking out, and my dad and Will are in there!"

As if conjured up by the mention of his name, Will strode out of the stable, a cell phone to his ear. "We need an ambulance," he said into it, and then paused, listening. "To Covington. Hurry." That's when his gaze met Kit's.

She tried to run past him, yelling, "Dad!" but Will grabbed her and held on, even when she struggled. "Dad!" she yelled again, thoughts of her mother flashing through her brain. *She's been gone a whole year, and it's been so horrible without her. And now Dad . . . no, not Dad, too . . . please, please no . . .*

Chapter 2

Kit paced nervously, trying to forget the last time she'd spent a whole night in a hospital. It had been when her mom . . . well . . . when *that* had happened.

Her logical brain knew that hospitals are designed to help people. They're places where doctors, nurses, and staff have to be able to do their jobs quickly and efficiently for the sake of their patients. But Kit's logical brain wasn't in charge at the moment. Her emotions had battered down her logic walls in tsunami waves, reducing her thoughts to a jumble of *I hate this place! Where's my dad? I hate this place! Is he okay? I hate this place! He has to be okay, he has to, he has to, and I hate this big, stupid, cold, sterile place!*

Will was the only person with her. Sally Warrington, one of Covington's English teachers, had driven them to the town hospital, but she had stayed downstairs in the main lobby to intercept any students or staff who came to show support for Kit and her father. Sally had also sent Will to wait with Kit for news of her father's condition. Kit shuddered to think that even her teacher realized that Will seemed to be a strong, comforting presence for her. He sat on one of the numerous plastic chairs in the emergency waiting room, his padded blue coat piled on his lap, his handsome face blank of expression.

"Why would somebody stuff all the Guys in the ceiling?" Kit muttered as she paced. "What kind of stupid idea was that?"

Leaning forward in his chair, his chin in his hands, Will recited:

"Remember, remember the fifth of November
Gunpowder, treason and plot.
I see no reason why gunpowder, treason
Should ever be forgot."

Kit looked at him. "What?"

Will seemed to come out of a trance. "Oh, um— it's a famous poem about the whole Guy Fawkes thing and the attempt to kill the king. I learned it when I was a kid. It just came to mind because, you know . . . the Guys falling out of the loft and all."

Kit nodded. The loud crashing noise that had started this whole disaster had been the trapdoor in the stable ceiling, the one that led to the hay-loft, falling open. Juniper Cottage hadn't really won the Covington Guy Fawkes competition after all. Someone had stolen all the Guys from all the other school houses and hidden them up in the hayloft so that Juniper Cottage could enjoy an easy win. Too bad whoever-it-was hadn't secured the latch properly.

Kit paced some more while Will sat glumly. "I need to know what's going on!" she finally griped at him, as if he could magically make the doctor appear but was choosing not to just to torture her.

Will grabbed a bag on the table next to him. "Do you want some crisps?"

Kit sighed and turned away.

"No?" Will gave a weak chuckle. "Sorry. That's ridiculous. So not what you need. They're prawn flavored."

"Eww, that's not a flavor—that's a punish-ment." Kit's response to the little joke slipped out automatically, sarcasm being a major Bridges family trait. What she really wanted to do was scream and maybe throw one of the ugly plastic chairs across the room. Yanking those cheap blinds off the window would vent some frustration, too, but she did none of those things. She just hugged herself tighter and turned farther away from Will.

He tried again for humor, shaking the crisps bag once and then setting it back on the table. "Well, at least you know where they are in case I say something idiotic again." The joke fell flat, so he added sincerely, "I just wish I could help."

Kit sat down next to him. "I'm so worried about Dad. What if he can't walk?"

"Come on, everything's going to be all right."

"I hope so. But his foot looked so messed up."

"Your dad's a really tough guy." Will stated it as a fact, a fact in which he clearly believed.

Kit appreciated that. She could always count on Will to tell her the truth, and right now, the truth meant everything. She usually hated being told that everything was going to be all right. Why did people always say that? *Don't worry—everything is going to be all right.* She'd heard it over and over when her mom had . . .

well. And things hadn't been all right, not for a very long time. And now they weren't all right all over again!

Yet here was Will, assuring her that, yes, things would turn out fine, that her dad was stronger than any little foot injury, and despite her own bleak outlook, she believed him. *Dad really is strong,* she thought. *In fact, when this is all over, I bet he'll go straight to the horse that stepped on his foot and step on him back.* A ridiculous idea—Rudy would never hurt a horse—but the idea of such a silly retribution lifted her spirits. "I just wish my mom was here," she admitted.

"Yeah."

Kit glanced at her watch. "You know, you don't have to stick around. Really. Miss Warrington said she'd drive you back."

"I want to stay, at least until we know something."

Kit smiled. She was so glad that Will wanted to stay with her. She wasn't quite sure what was happening with their odd relationship. It felt like it was growing into something more than friendship, but exactly what, she couldn't yet say. She had hopes, though.

For some reason, that reminded her that her dad hadn't been the only victim when the Guys had fallen out of the hayloft. "Are the horses okay?"

Will nodded. "Yeah, they're fine. A little bit spooked, and Thunder got a little nick on his fetlock, but they're fine."

"I can't believe someone would stuff all the Guys in the ceiling," Kit said for probably the nineteenth time. "I mean, who would—?"

"Hey, Kit?" It was the voice of Rudy Bridges as he appeared through the doors in a wheelchair pushed by a nurse.

Kit leaped to her feet. "Dad!" She threw her arms around him and squeezed with all her might.

"What are you two doing here?" Rudy said around the mass of distraught daughter clinging to his neck. "It's late. You should both be in bed."

Kit kept hugging him. "Miss Warrington brought us over while you were in the ambulance." The pressure of held-back tears strained her voice. "What did they say?"

"I'd tell you, Kit, but I can't breathe." Rudy gave her a fatherly pat on the back before gently peeling her off.

"Sorry," Kit said, standing straight again. "I'm just worried." She continued to grip his hands, afraid of losing physical contact.

He gave her a reassuring smile. "I just have to have one more X-ray to see if I need surgery."

At that, Will said, "Oh, no. Mr. Bridges, I'm so sorry."

"It's not your fault, son," Rudy said. "Why don't you two head home? It's going to be a long night for me, so there's no sense in it being a long night for you, too."

Kit looked at him as if he'd gone nuts, or as her British friends put it, gone mad. "I'm not going anywhere!"

"I think she means that, sir," said Will.

"Yeah," Rudy sighed in defeat.

Kit smiled, glad that her father was accepting the facts. A two-thousand-pound Clydesdale horse couldn't have pulled her away from him now.

"Well, then," Rudy said to Will, "why don't you head home with Miss Sally?" He politely informed his nurse, "My daughter's going to come with us. There's really no point in arguing with her."

The nurse nodded with a knowing smile and started pushing Rudy's wheelchair to the door that led to Radiology. Kit fetched her coat and turned to Will. "Thank you for being so helpful."

Even as she hurried after her dad, Kit noticed that a strange look had come over Will's face.

When her father was wheeled into the X-ray room, Kit automatically followed.

"I'm sorry," the nurse told her, "but you can't go in." When Kit gave her a blank stare, the nurse jerked her thumb at the sign on the door. "X-rays? You do know they're a form of radiation, right?"

"Oh! Right. Yeah. Sorry." Kit was directed to another waiting room, where she sat down in yet another hard plastic chair. She let out a long, slow breath.

Now that she knew her dad was going to be okay, exhaustion hit her like a sledgehammer. *No, I can't get sleepy yet*, she thought, and bought a cup of really terrible coffee from a vending machine around the corner. After letting it cool, she downed it in three gulps and tossed the cup into the trash.

All the things that were happening to her—they weren't anything like what she'd expected when she'd first come to The Covington Academy for the Equestrian Arts mere months ago. Her move from

Montana to England had happened so fast! She'd barely had time to adjust to all the changes before classes had started. She had made new friends, true, but she still missed her old ones, especially Charlie.

What is he doing right now? she wondered, and pulled out her cell phone to check the time. It was 1:04 in the morning, which meant it was 6:04 in the evening in Montana. *He's eating dinner with his family,* she thought. *Let me guess . . . meat loaf with ketchup, corn on the cob, and a side dish made with some kind of beans. Oh, and if Charlie's lucky, cupcakes for dessert. Strawberry frosting, of course.*

Thinking about dinner "back home" made her think of her mother. *Mom, if you were still alive, you, me, and Dad would still be back in our house together, happy. I could still talk to you and go places with you and*—she laughed softly—*and even help you with the housework. And I wouldn't always feel like my heart was in pieces. And I wouldn't have to wait here in this awful hospital all alone. I wouldn't even* be *in this hospital.*

Then again, if she hadn't come to England, she wouldn't have met TK.

He was just a horse, a silly, irritating, beautiful, stubborn, dancing horse. Kit still didn't understand the connection she had with TK, but it was there, and she knew that TK could feel it, too. Somehow they belonged together. Why? She didn't know. But her growing love for the black gelding had been enough to help her overcome her fear of riding, a fear born when she'd fallen off her childhood horse, Freckles. Her foot had caught in the stirrup, and she had been dragged. *I was never going to ride a horse again*, she thought, *but TK changed all that. I rode him! Just a little, but I did it!* And she was determined to do more.

But now this awful accident had happened, and TK, along with all the other horses, had been badly scared. TK was an especially skittish horse with unusually delicate sensibilities. It would take time to earn his trust again. Kit vowed to do whatever she could to help him. *We're a team*, she thought, yawning again. *TK will be all right. And Dad's foot will heal up just fine, and we'll all be okay.*

Just one question remained: Who put all the Guys in the hayloft?

Chapter 3

TRUTH AND DIRE CONSEQUENCES

Will drove back to Covington with Sally. He quietly slipped into the dorm room he shared with Navarro Andrada to find Nav in bed and asleep, though he had thoughtfully left Will's lamp on. This was good because Will stored most of his clothes and other belongings all over the floor in random heaps. He probably would have tripped on his first step into the room. But it also meant that Nav was wearing a black satin sleep mask to block the lamplight, which made him look like a snoozing bandit.

Will smiled at his refined roomie's habits and climbed into bed, clothes, coat, and all. He kicked off his boots from there and snuggled into his pillow. It would have been nice to fall asleep at that point.

It was only one thirty in the morning, so there was plenty of time to rest up for the coming day. But for a long time all he could do was lie there, eyes open, battling with his guilt.

Will woke to Nav shaking his shoulders. "Get up!" Nav hissed. "Red alert! Ducasse just saw Lady Covington heading this way, and I'm sure you know why!"

Will jumped out of bed like a spark from a fire. He pulled off his coat and clothes and began to yank on his school uniform as Nav dressed, too, all the while giving a recitation of all the things they should *not* have done lately—like steal all the Guy Fawkes dummies and hide them in the hayloft. "It may have started as a funny way to win the competition, but it's gone way too far now," Nav concluded. "Who knows what Lady C will do to us?"

"Worrying about a punishment is always worse than the actual punishment," Will assured him.

Nav shot him a sidelong frown. "You would know."

There came a knock at the door, and the boys of Juniper Cottage spilled into the room, all of them looking like they were about to face a firing squad. "She's coming!" Josh announced as if they didn't know already.

"Lady C?" Will checked. "Okay, just calm down—"

"But th-th-th-th . . ." Josh stammered for a moment, unable to get a word out, he was so frantic. "There's no time!" he finally blurted out. "How much is a flight to Vegas? Wait, what am I talking about? Nav, dude!" He pointed at Nav. "Your family jet, right? It makes sense! It's easier!"

Nav rolled his eyes.

"No one person takes the blame, okay?" Will told the group, trying to rekindle their camaraderie before Josh's freak-out had them all leaping out the windows. "All for one and one for all."

"Keep it together, guys," added Nav in his best tone of authority.

They all promptly froze in place when someone *tap-tap-tapped* on the door. Will remained calm, though he saw Josh rub sweaty palms against his trousers and Nav shove his fists into his uniform jacket pockets. The door then opened to reveal Lady Covington, headmistress of The Covington Academy for the Equestrian Arts.

She was a tall aristocratic woman, more handsome than pretty, and she was dressed in her usual neat business skirt suit and heels. Her ginger hair was styled in its customary French twist, and she wore a single string of pearls around her neck. It seemed to Will that all the women he knew wore pearl necklaces. He found himself hoping for just an instant that Kit Bridges would never, ever own a single pearl. Pearls were so *not* her.

"Gentlemen," Lady Covington greeted them in her crisp, dignified voice. It sounded to Will perhaps a little more crisp and dignified than usual. "I will be quick and to the point. Clearly someone from Juniper Cottage was responsible for last night's incident. You had the only viable Guy entry. The guilty party or parties has until tomorrow morning to confess."

Will noticed that, for all his usual bluster, Josh suddenly stared down at his toes. One by one, the other boys did, too. Will did not. He kept his gaze steadily on Lady Covington as she continued. "However, if no one steps forward to do the right thing, every single member of this house will face the consequences. And I assure you, they will be dire."

Nobody moved.

"Will!" Lady Covington snapped, grimacing at the mess on the floor.

"Ma'am!" Will responded.

"Muck out this room immediately. Good morning, gentlemen." And she left.

"Wh-what happened?" Josh said, shaking his head. "I think I blacked out."

Later that morning, the tack room was filled with Fourth-Form students waiting for the start of Rudy Bridges's riding class. He hadn't arrived yet, however, so everyone was busy gossiping about the events of the previous night.

Kit and Anya, on the other hand, were talking about romance, specifically the evolving relationship between Kit and Will. "When it started to rain, we just stood in the doorway of the refreshment tent and ate s'mores," Kit told Anya, trying to make it all sound very matter-of-fact. "Let's see . . ." She pretended to have trouble recalling details that were, in fact, burned forever into her memory. "I told him I loved bonfire night, and he agreed, and we both got chocolate all over our faces."

"And that's when you kissed!" Anya broke in. "Mmmm, chocolate kisses."

Kit laughed. "No, we just wiped the chocolate off," she corrected Anya, trying to hide how dreamy the scene had actually been. The bonfire had kept blazing even when the rain had started, and sparks had danced through the air like tiny magical fireworks. The taste of the s'mores had been like velvet heaven, and Will's warm blue eyes had gazed directly into hers as they'd oh-so-slowly moved closer and closer—

"And?" Anya prompted.

Kit realized she'd gone silent. "Oh. Uh, and I thanked him for helping me to ride TK, and he said you're welcome."

"Wait. Go back to the kissing part. Where were you? *When* were you? Ohhh, tell me everything!" She was whispering, but her breathy voice held enough excitement for three people. "Oh, my gosh, I'm hyperventilating!"

"Anya, you can't just stop breathing every time you get excited," Kit advised her friend with amusement. "Otherwise you're going to drop dead the next time you see a puppy. And"—she shrugged—"we didn't kiss."

Anya shook her head. "La la la la la, can't hear you! In my world, you totally kissed. Twice!"

"Not quite. Elaine called Will over with some question or another, and that, as they say, was that."

"No!" Anya bleated. "How dare Elaine—?"

"Shhhh! I'm sure she didn't do it on purpose."

"Oh, she *so* did!"

Anya was right. Kit had noticed Elaine spying on her and Will right before they'd been about to kiss, so of course she'd put a stop to it. But Kit didn't want to think about it. It made her want to punch things. "Whatev. We had a good time. And then . . . you know, later . . . Will came to the hospital and waited with me." Kit marveled at how her time with Will during the bonfire still seemed like it was happening. Just talking about it put goose bumps on her arms all over again. But their mutual wait at the hospital already felt like it had happened a week ago. In a way, Kit wished it had. The further away in time the hospital was, the better.

All discussion stopped when Kit heard the distinct step-*clunk* step-*clunk* of her dad approaching. The doctors had placed Rudy's right foot in a big walking boot, practically a cast except it was designed to take pressure so that Rudy could walk. A cast would have required him to use crutches. As it was, he had to use a cane. He'd also been given medication for pain. Being the stubborn old-fashioned cowboy that he was, Rudy had complained about the cane and refused to take the medication.

Kit watched him hobble into the tack room. He was leaning on Will, who made sure his teacher didn't fall flat on his face. Kit carefully studied her dad's expression — he looked annoyed but not too much, which meant that he'd given in and taken at least some of the medication. *Good,* she thought. *Über-grumpy dad-teacher plus classmates with camera phones can only spell a social media disaster.* She didn't think she could take one of those right now, and her dad definitely couldn't.

"Good morning," Rudy greeted them, step-*clunking* into place. "The doctors tell me I'll live. But before we move on, I want you all to think about what happened on bonfire night." Rudy's expression hardened. "Those horses are our responsibility, and we failed them." He let that sink in, then continued, "Now, a spooked horse can be dangerous, so even if you think he's your best friend, take it easy the next few days, yeah?"

Kit felt like those last words had been directed at her. Well, she wasn't going to let her dad or TK down ever again, starting today. Starting right now.

Elaine stepped forward. "Are we forgetting that someone is responsible for Mr. Bridges getting hurt?" she asked the class, sounding more like a peeved adult than Rudy did. "Did anyone think about that?"

"I appreciate the sentiment, Elaine," Rudy began, "but I'm not—"

"His foot is in a cast," Elaine barged on. "He is completely useless. How will we ever prepare for the Covington House Cup now?"

Kit held her breath in shock. Elaine had actually called her dad *useless*!

Rudy got as far as "I am not—" before Elaine interrupted him again, fetching a stool.

"Take a seat, you poor man. You have had a difficult night." She placed it directly behind him as if expecting him to dramatically collapse onto it.

Rudy's ego seemed to have had enough. "I am not so banged up that I cannot teach a class," he declared.

Uh-oh, there it is, Kit thought. *Elaine poked him square in his ego. Now he's going to be grumpy no matter how good or bad he feels.* She sighed. *Thanks, Elaine.*

Recalling her interrupted moment with Will, she added, *Again*.

"Everyone, out into the ring," Rudy ordered, and he stepped toward the door, putting weight on his injured foot. As everyone watched, pain blossomed on his face and he had to pull back.

Nobody moved.

"*Now*," Rudy snapped. He grabbed his Stetson from Will and forced himself to hobble out of the room on his own, his teeth gritted and his pride seeming just barely intact.

The rest of the students silently followed, including Kit. She badly wanted to visit TK, but more than that, she wanted to get away from Elaine. Why was Miss Perfect so concerned about her dad's health, anyway?

Elaine filed out of the tack room behind the Juniper Cottage students—Nav, Will, and Josh. She stopped them halfway down the stable corridor. "So. Juniper Cottage," she said in a slightly threatening manner.

Nav, Will, and Josh turned around.

"You made this personal when you put *my* horse

in danger," Elaine told them. "Never, ever get between a girl and her horse. Whoever did this will be caught, and the consequences will be dire."

Josh smirked at Nav. "Why are the consequences here always so *dire*?"

The comment made Elaine zero in on him. "Joshua, I think you and I should chat first. Meet me after class." She marched away.

"Oh, man," Josh grumbled. "I cannot deal with her. She's like a cold Lady C! I mean, I know I come off as the bad boy of Juniper Cottage—"

"To who?" Will quipped.

Josh frowned.

"Relax, boys," Nav said. "I know exactly how to handle her."

Kit leaned up against TK's closed stall door, staring at him. He was facing away from her, his head tucked into the far corner. He would have looked kind of cute that way, like a pouting little boy, if circumstances weren't so awful.

Everyone else in Kit's riding class had just completed a series of simple exercises out in the practice ring to reinforce the horse-and-rider connection. The horses all behaved well despite having had such a terrifying night—except for TK. He had refused to come out of his stall, so Kit had spent the entire class period standing with her dad outside the ring. Normally it would have been embarrassing, but mostly she had just felt anxious about TK.

Now that class was over, he was still ignoring her.

"Come on, boy," she called in her sweetest voice. "It's cool. You're cool. Come on over here and see Kit." *Terrific*, she thought. *I'm referring to myself in the third person.* She held up a fistful of treats. "I brought you some mega-yummy snacks!"

TK didn't move a muscle, and Kit was so engrossed in getting his attention that she didn't notice Will enter the stable behind her.

She frowned. "Now you're making it look like I'm talking to myself. Come on, boy—save me!"

Nothing.

Kit turned around in defeat and found Will staring at her. She noticed that his expression was somewhat anguished, but she was too wrapped up in her own present dilemma to wonder about it. "He won't even come near me," she said. "I thought he trusted me."

"He does," said Will. "You're his person."

"I just barely managed to ride him before the bonfire. What if he won't let me do it again, and I can't save him?" Kit waited for the perfect words, the exact words that Will always seemed to say at the exact time that Kit needed to hear them.

Instead, she got an "Um." Then Will gulped. "I need a pitchfork," he muttered, and hurried away.

Kit couldn't help but feel bad for him. *This has been hard on all of us*, she thought. *And now he's got a ton of work to do, fixing all the damage the spooked horses did, kicking in their stalls. Still . . .* She peered back into TK's stall, where the sign that had been tacked up since she arrived still hung:

UNPREDICTABLE AND DANGEROUS.
KEEP GATE SHUT — HORSE WILL BOLT

TK didn't seem very dangerous right now. Kit imagined that if he were to move at all, he would just shuffle farther into the corner. "Come on, buddy," she urged him. "Hey. It's me. Your person."

TK remained motionless.

Will felt lousy. He meandered down the dining corridor thinking of all the repercussions of his one dumb decision. It was a long list. He'd let his friends in Juniper Cottage down by not latching the hayloft door correctly in his haste to get the Guys hidden. He'd let the horses down when the loft door had banged open. He'd let Mr. Bridges down by creating circumstances that had gotten him injured. And only moments ago, he'd let Kit down by running away from her when she needed him, just because he felt guilty. TK was an odd horse, to be sure, but Will knew plenty of tricks that might have helped Kit get his attention in a calm, controlled way. But no, he'd muttered something stupid about pitchforks and made a run for it. How cowardly. How—

"William," came a peppy female voice, "I understand you're assisting Mr. Bridges." It was Miss Warrington, and she was practically hopping on her toes as she asked, "How is he?"

"Yeah," said Will absently. "He's getting around. Slowly."

"Such a shock," she said. "I'll stop in later, but, um, could you possibly deliver something to him? From me?" She unslung a large cooler bag from her shoulder and handed it over.

Will, often confused by the chirpy young teacher's behavior, took the bag, wondering why she couldn't deliver it herself. Probably busy grading papers or something. "Okay," he promised her.

Sally beamed a wide smile. "Cheers!" she said in thanks.

Chapter 4

SHERTOCK HONES MEETS MEAT LOAF MUSH

The Guy Fawkes investigation was under way.

Elaine stood at a table in the student lounge with Peaches perched primly in a chair beside her. They had already shooed everyone else out of the room. Elaine wanted no distractions and especially no interlopers. She was going to maintain complete control over these proceedings because it was a matter of school justice—and a little bit of revenge.

Elaine liked revenge.

"In order to solve this Guy Fawkes travesty, I'll have to embrace my inner Sherlock Holmes," she announced to Peaches. "And you, Peaches, are to be my Watson."

Peaches's wide brown eyes held no understanding whatsoever. "Your what-son?" she asked in her thick Eastern European accent. "Who's Shertock Hones?"

Sometimes Elaine wondered why she tolerated Peaches at all. The girl was a total bunny-nosed goofball of a person, easily distracted by shiny objects and never quite in sync with what was happening around her. Elaine found her quite vexing at times. Then again, Peaches was loyal, and she did whatever Elaine told her to do. Yes, that was probably why Peaches remained Elaine's number one henchman.

"Who is Sherlock Holmes?" Elaine repeated in surprise. "Peaches! The world's most famous detective?"

Peaches took a moment to think hard. She shook her blond head. "Nope."

Elaine tried again. "Benedict Cumberbatch?" Surely the girl watched TV.

But Peaches giggled at the actor's name, her pretty face scrunching up in amusement, creating a cute little dimple in the center of her chin. "What is that?" She laughed.

"Peaches, this is precisely why you should never speak." Elaine heaved a great sigh. Good help was so hard to find. "All right, this is how it works. You will be the friendly good cop and lull our suspects into a false sense of security. Then I come in full force as the bad cop and ta-da! We get our confession!"

She studied the six large cards arranged on the table before her. She had prepared them that morning, conducting research into all six boys of Juniper Cottage and reducing that information into easy-to-compare data cards. The cards were laminated, of course. Elaine liked to laminate all her papers and reports, including her daily class notes. That way, everything remained clean and tidy even if it was handled roughly. This investigation was going to be rough indeed, so lamination had been essential.

Each card displayed each suspect's school photo, name, residence, and country of origin. Most important, Elaine had included a spot for each suspect's alibi, all of which were uncertain at this point, hence her investigation.

Being a creative person, Elaine had decorated the cards, too, placing the famous silhouette of Sherlock Holmes on the bottom and a picture of a magnifying glass on the top, flanked by question marks, and she had designed a neat border of little fingerprints all around the edges. If these cards had been a class assignment, she would have gotten a perfect mark. Naturally.

"Let's begin with our weakest link," she said. "The ever-shifty Joshua."

At the same time, just outside the student lounge door, Nav sprawled on a comfy couch. It was there to give visitors a place to rest as they toured the building, but Nav was there to support Josh, who was waiting to be called in for questioning by Elaine. Josh was pacing back and forth in such an annoying display of uncontrolled heebie-jeebies that it was making Nav want to nail his friend's shoes to one spot.

"If it were anyone else, I could deal," Joshua babbled as he paced. "But it's Elaine! You know she doesn't fall for the same stuff that other people fall for!"

"So don't talk to her," Nav suggested.

Josh shook his head. "Makes it too suspicious."

"Look, just stick to the plan, and you'll be fine. Just deny, deny, deny, then send her my way."

The door opened. "Joshuaaaa," Peaches sang out as if she were calling a child in for a surprise party.

Josh saw who it was. "It's only Peaches," he told Nav with relief. "I got this."

He plastered a fake smile on and strode confidently through the door. But when he saw who was sitting at the table inside the student lounge, his smile fizzed out. "I don't got this," he said, making eye contact with Elaine. "I don't got this!" He spun on his heel and fled like a mouse from a cat.

"You won't get away with this!" Elaine yelled after him. "We will find you!"

This was Nav's cue. He lazily pushed himself up from the couch and sauntered in, closing the door with a casual push of a finger. "My apologies," he said, taking the seat opposite Elaine. "Josh is feeling a little under the weather."

"We are *so* not done with him," Elaine said. "What about you? Are you ready to spill?"

Before Nav could think up a suave reply, Peaches leaned toward him and said, "I'm the good cop."

Nav grinned. "Oh, yes, Peaches. I can tell."

"But you need to watch out for Elaine," Peaches went on. "She is Detective Cucumber Patch."

"Cucumber Patch?" Nav repeated, puzzled. Then his inner lie generator burst into gear and he said, "Oh, *Cumberbatch*! Of course! I know the family well. In fact, it was Phineas Cumberbatch who first introduced me to polo! I think it was at their summer place in Argentina." He faked a hearty laugh. "Oh, I shudder to think how pitiful I must have been that first time!" As he spoke, the false incident was growing so vivid in his mind that Nav actually imagined himself falling off a horse while trying to play polo outside a huge mansion in the rugged Argentine hills.

Peached giggled at his story, but Elaine looked like she had heard enough. "You're deflecting. Watson might fall for it, but I will not."

Peaches immediately stopped giggling.

Nav accepted defeat graciously. He had a better strategy ready anyway. "Let's be frank. I had nothing to do with stealing any Guys. Although it does pain me to have to tell you . . ." He paused for effect.

"Get to the point," Elaine snapped.

Nav leaned forward and whispered, "I did notice

Leo Ducasse sneaking out of both Snapdragon Cottage and Birch House earlier that day."

"Leo?" Elaine said.

Nine minutes later: "Nav said that?"

Leo Ducasse sat in the same chair that Nav had vacated, facing Detective Cucumber Patch and Watson, both of whom stared soberly back at him.

"No, no, no," he went on in his French accent, denying the accusation. "But," he added, lowering his voice, "I did see Alex Taylor carrying something in a huge equipment bag."

"Alex?" Elaine said.

Seven minutes later: "No," Alex Taylor protested. "Take your questions to Wyatt Blain. He claims he hurt his arm during warm-up, but it happened during the fire."

"Wyatt?" Elaine said.

Four minutes later: "Will," declared Wyatt Blain. "Find Will."

Forty seconds later: Wyatt exited the student lounge, leaving Watson and Elaine alone to ponder the staggering amount of information they *hadn't* gotten. They had heard a lot of stories, but none of them offered any real facts or led to any solid conclusions.

"Oh, I'm so confused," moaned Peaches.

"How shocking," Elaine commented cruelly. As usual, Peaches didn't catch the insult. Elaine picked up the last of her cards: Will and Josh. "Two more left. And failure is not in the cards."

Currently oblivious to his sought-after status, Will delivered Sally's cooler bag to Rudy in the tack room, as requested. He set it on the desk and proceeded to pull out several plastic containers while Rudy, leaning on the edge of a smaller work desk with his arms folded, watched.

"What's in that one?" Rudy asked as Will pulled out the largest container.

Will tipped it one way, then the other, trying to identify the sloshy substance inside. "Maybe it's . . . food?" He laughed.

"Oh, yeah, you're really selling it." Rudy moved forward to take a look, seeming to forget about his injured foot. The second he stepped down on it, he stumbled, barely catching himself on the larger desk before falling. He groaned in pain.

"Whoa!" said Will. "Are you all right?"

"Yeah, I'm . . ." Rudy let Will help him to his chair. "I think I may have pushed it a little this afternoon."

Trying to be helpful, Will set the big container in front of his teacher. "Here, try this," he suggested, removing the lid. When the smell hit him, he blurted out, "Or not."

Rudy peered at the whatever-it-was with genuine puzzlement. "Is that meat loaf? Why is it so watery?" He offered it to Will. "Here, I dare you."

"No, I'm, uh . . ." The smell hit Will again, and he held up a hand. "I'm a vegetarian?" Actually, the maybe meat loaf didn't smell all that bad. It was the way it looked that made his stomach turn, almost like the mess poor Thunder made after he'd had too many treats last month. And, okay, the smell really *was* bad. Why on earth had Sally put *cinnamon* in meat loaf? The prankster side of Will couldn't help it—he was dying to see Rudy try some. "Oh, come on, sir, you need to get your strength back up," he urged.

Rudy made a skeptical face but spooned up a couple of suspicious meatlike chunks and put them in his mouth. Will counted to two before Rudy gagged and spit them back out.

Still feeling helpless and confused by TK's strange behavior, as if the entire earth were rotating without them, Kit entered her math classroom. Anya was with her, trying to lift her spirits with nonstop cheerful chatter. "What if we wallpaper our ceiling in pictures?" she suggested. "Wouldn't that be fun?"

Kit automatically headed to her desk. "Yeah, ceiling paper—sounds great."

Anya waved her hand in Kit's face. "Hello! Earth to Kit?"

It finally dawned on Kit that she was being really rude to her friend. "Sorry," she said. "I can't stop thinking about TK." She moved to sit, and her eyes landed on a yellow sticky note on her desktop. She picked it up and read it. "And I'm not the only one," she said, smiling for the first time that day.

"What's that?"

Kit turned the paper so that Anya could read it. It said, *Have fun. Let TK come to you.*

"Ooooh, it's so intriguing," said Anya. "I wonder who wrote it."

Kit wondered, too. She didn't recognize the handwriting, and the message was too short for her to get a sense of the writer's identity. She glanced around the classroom, still smiling. *Somebody cares*, she thought. *Somebody wants to help me and TK! But why are they being so mysterious about it?*

Early the next morning, Elaine wandered the hallways before the first class bell, hunting for her final suspects. She spotted Will and stepped right in his path. She knew how sneaky he could be. Sneaky and cute. Really cute. But now was not the time to notice such things.

"I need to talk to you straightaway," she said, using her best authoritative tone.

Will broke out in a heart-melting smile. "Hey! Your hair looks really nice! Did you do something new with it?"

A compliment, and such a personal one, was the last thing Elaine expected. She paused, blushing, and stroked her long ponytail. Will had never complimented her hair before, which was strange because she always wore it this way. She found herself growing warm, pleased that she'd managed to wear her hair the way he liked all this time without even knowing it.

Will looked embarrassed. "Oh, sorry. What was your question?"

How odd. Elaine had no idea what she'd been about to say. She racked her brain, trying to remember. "Culprit . . ." she murmured, and then it came back to her. "Oh! Um, the Guy Fawkes . . . thing. You wouldn't be the one responsible, would you?"

"Oh, no way," Will replied. "No, I wouldn't want to wreck your bonfire night." He smiled again and started to leave, then turned back. "Josh looked rather sketchy," he offered. "More so than usual, I mean."

Elaine accepted the tip with a vague nod. Oh, that smile of his . . . She felt dizzy, but there was something so pleasant about it that she simply watched Will walk away, admiring how nicely he moved, like one of those famous Lipizzaner stallions that could trot so stylishly while never seeming to touch the ground.

She resumed her way down the corridor, thinking that maybe it was time to give the ends of her hair a bit of a trim and try that fancy new shampoo. . . .

English class ended, leaving Josh to wish he had some kind of futuristic science-fiction teleporter-type thingy. That way he could just *pop!* out of the room and avoid Elaine.

He knew she was looking for him. He knew that the minute he stepped out the door, she would appear, probably in a puff of black smoke. He could practically feel her out there waiting to catch him in her cold iron grasp. She would wrest the truth from him, and he would be defenseless to stop her. Why? Simple. She gave him the creeps. She was just too perfect and prepared for even the tiniest events. She laminated everything within a six-mile reach. Worst of all, she didn't think his jokes were funny.

Yup, something was definitely wrong with her.

But facts were facts: he had to leave the classroom at some point. So he got up and trudged to the door, only to jump back when Peaches popped in, chirping, "Good cop!"

When Elaine appeared behind her, Josh really jumped back. "It almost feels like you've been avoiding us," Elaine commented.

Again Josh wished he had that teleporter. Maybe he could find the next best thing. *Come on, secret passageway!* Covington was an old school. Maybe there was a secret door somewhere that would lead to a hidden refuge, like old catacombs lit by torches or better yet, a cave with a stone door that had a guardian genie who would protect him from anyone who freaked him out—in other words, Elaine.

He threw himself at the nearest wall, patting it and poking the wall phone unit, desperately looking for the salvation that he knew wasn't there. "What's the point of having a fancy old castle if there are no secret passageways?" he grumbled, knowing he was just wasting time. That was the whole point, wasn't it? Delay, delay, delay, and try to avoid all unpleasantness until it went away.

Unfortunately, unpleasantness *didn't* usually go away. Present example: Elaine was still there.

"We need to talk about the Guy Fawkes incident," she said, closing in on him. Peaches closed in with her, but Peaches was just too cute to appear properly menacing.

Taking comfort in that, Josh sank into a nearby chair. "Look, I'm telling you right now, you have the wrong dude, okay? The only *foxes* I know are the two foxes right in front of me so . . ."

"Aww!" Peaches said, seeming pleased by the compliment.

Elaine rolled her eyes. "Don't even try to use that maple-syrupy charm on us. Look, if you didn't do it, then tell us who did."

Josh froze. Looking into Elaine's eyes was like gazing into a nightmare. "Um . . . I forget."

"This could all be over now, Joshua. You just need to say a name."

"Just a name. Um . . ." Josh scrambled for some way, *any* way, to stall some more. "Alex," he muttered. "Wyatt . . . ? Who was I supposed to . . . ? Uhh . . . can we go back to the good cop Peaches? 'Cause she kind of reminds me of those old lady-cop shows that my gran liked." When Elaine's glare grew darker, which should have been impossible but such was his luck, Josh said, "Yeah, okay, fine, I liked them, too, but, like, they're awesome, right? And—"

"Tell. Us. NOW," Elaine said, getting in his face.

Josh couldn't take it. Those nightmare eyes! She was going to laminate him any second! "It was Will!" he shouted. Getting ahold of himself, he repeated in a more normal voice, "It was Will."

A strange look crossed Elaine's face at this news. She stepped back. "Thank you. You've been very helpful. Excuse me." And she left.

Now that her nightmare eyes were off him, Josh regained what little courage he possessed. He sprinted to the door and called after her, "You can't do this! There will be consequences! *Dire* ones!" He gave a frustrated, "Argh!" and frowned at Peaches. "I'm weak, Peaches. So weak."

She gave him a sweet, understanding look. "It is better you told her. Now she won't make me abduct you in the night." With that, Peaches hurried after her boss, leaving Josh to ponder her parting words. . . .

Kit entered the tack room with Anya in tow. "Hey, Dad! I have a proper English breakfast courtesy of Sally." She handed him a small cooler bag.

Rudy shuddered. "Ugh! More? Forget it." He handed the bag back. "Feed it to Ducky."

As much as her dad's *ugh* response surprised Kit, the idea of offering the food to Ducky did not. Anya's horse, Just Ducky, or Ducky for short, was well known for eating absolutely anything you put in front of him. His favorites included crackers, watermelon, and sour gummy candies, but he was not by any means discerning. Anya occasionally worried that he might get sick from it, but as they say, everything came out all right in the end.

Everything was not all right now, though. "That's not very nice," Kit said to Rudy. After all, Sally had gone to a lot of trouble to make the food. When she had asked Kit to deliver it for her, Kit had seen how much it meant to her. Sally was obviously concerned that Rudy get the best nutrition possible so that his foot would heal well. The school depended on him. But he was refusing it, just like that?

"You want not nice?" Rudy asked. "Tell her not to cook again. Like, ever. Forever and ever."

Kit wasn't going to let him get away with being so rude. "Ooh, look at me," she said in a bad imitation of her father. "I'm Rudy, the rough, tough cowboy. I don't like when nice ladies are nice to me."

Rudy sighed.

Hm, not enough response, Kit thought. *I've got to hit him harder.* She turned to Anya. "Come on, Anya. Join in."

Anya squirmed uncomfortably. "I can't," she said. "He's a teacher!"

Doing her best Anya imitation, Kit said primly, "You would have me poke fun at an instructor? Oh, I couldn't possibly! Oh, my heavens!"

That did it. Anya struck a sassy pose and, in a dreadful American accent, said to Rudy, "I'm Mr. Bridges, and I am understandably miffed because I got injured and now I can't do my job to the best of my abilities." She ended the speech with a growly "Huh!"

Everyone — including Rudy — burst out laughing. It was so out of character for Anya! Kit was pleased to see her loosen up so much, and to hear her home country's accent butchered so badly in the process only made it funnier.

"You nailed it, Anya!" Kit giggled.

Rudy surrendered to the teens. "Okay, okay, I'm being ridiculous."

"And ungrateful," added Kit.

Rudy nodded. "And grouchy."

"And mean," Kit said.

"All right, you can stop now," Rudy advised his daughter. "I'm starting to feel better."

Mission accomplished! Kit thought happily. True, the breakfast had been rejected, but Rudy was smiling, and that meant the world to Kit. "See you this aft," she told him, using her signature shorthand, and headed for the door with the cooler.

Rudy stopped her. "Where are you going with that?"

"I'm taking it to Ducky," Kit replied. "And then I'm going to tell Sally that you looooved it."

Rudy gave her a lopsided grin. "Smooth."

As the girls made their exit, Anya tried out her American accent again. "Hi, I'm Kit! I use my bed for jumping, and I eat chocolate for breakfast, duuuude!"

Kit laughed. "Well, it *is* true."

And then she got it. From out of the blue, she suddenly understood what her mysterious note writer was trying to tell her. "Oh! *That's* what the note meant! *Just have fun!*"

She started running, followed by Anya.

Chapter 5

A STABLE FULL OF SECRETS

Kit was prepared for Operation Happy Horse.

She led Anya to the stables and went straight to TK's stall. She opened the door wide.

It was as if the black gelding hadn't moved a muscle since the day before—he still stood with his head in the far corner, looking droopy. The sight made Kit's heart hurt, but she was sure her plan would work. Throwing all the happy energy she could muster into her voice and gestures, she said, "Come on, my friend! I reeeally miss you! Let's just hang out— no strings."

TK's left ear flicked.

"Perhaps the gentleman would like a shiny new apple!" Anya suggested, also injecting her voice with positive energy. She handed Kit the biggest, shiniest apple they'd been able to find in the kitchen.

"Oh, very nice!" said Kit, holding it out to TK.

He didn't respond.

"Come on, dude! It's just good manners to accept."

TK whinnied into the corner as if to say, "Nope, I'm not gonna move."

Kit let her apple-laden arm drop.

"Time for phase two?" Anya asked.

Kit nodded. "Phase two."

The girls turned to Nav, who was busy in the next stall grooming his bay gelding, Prince. "Hey, Nav," Kit greeted him. "Are you busy? We could use a hand. See, I'm trying to *have fun* and let TK *come to me*, and I think you and Prince would be a big help." She watched Nav carefully, wondering if he might be her mysterious note writer. If he was, he surely would recognize his own phrases.

Nav seemed surprised by the request but pleased. "Of course. Anything."

His response left Kit unsure as to whether he was the note writer, but it allowed her to begin Operation Happy Horse in earnest.

First she, Anya, and Nav ran around in front of TK's open stall, flailing all of their limbs around wildly. Kit leaped up and down, waving pieces of hay while Nav carried Anya around piggyback style as she beat him with a twig. Then Kit and Anya skipped back and forth, arm in arm, hooting and hollering in glee, while Nav walked Prince after them in an attempt to show TK that Prince thought all the fun was pretty exciting and maybe he should join in. All of them forced their laughter at first, trying to ignite TK's curiosity, but the goofier they acted, the more their laughter became real.

Then came the carrot dance. Waving long carrots that they'd nicked from the kitchen, the three students pranced around in front of TK, yelling, "Mmm, look at these yummy carrots!" and tickling one another with the long, floppy green carrot tops. Nav made a great show of eating one of them, chewing and making loud "Mmmm!" noises while staring straight at TK. Then they used the carrots as swords and pretended to duel with them, Nav calling out, "*En garde*, TK!"

At this point, they at least had TK's attention. He had swung his big head around and was watching, ears forward, probably wondering if they'd gone mad. That was good, though—just what Kit wanted. His curiosity was piqued. Now it was time for phase three.

"How about we go outside and play a game of tag?" Kit laughed with her friends, and they all dashed outside with Prince, making sure that TK watched as they left. They made as much noise as possible in the open stable courtyard, chasing one another with a lot more whooping and hollering.

"Kit!" Nav tapped her shoulder and pointed to the stable doorway.

TK was standing there.

"I think somebody else might want to have a turn at being it," Nav said.

Overwhelmed with joy, Kit hurried to TK, but not so fast that she might scare him away. "Thanks for coming out, boy," she said, petting his nose. "I missed you."

Anya watched from the side, happy to see Kit so relieved. She herself had a close relationship with her chestnut gelding, Ducky, but not like Kit and TK. She and Ducky were more like a two-person sports team, joined by the joy of performing in the ring. Ducky was talented. He was a show-off, too. It made Anya's job easier that he always did his best simply because he liked to. But they weren't heart-to-heart buddies, at least not like Kit and TK.

As Anya thought about Ducky while watching Kit and TK's reunion, Josh ambled over to her. "Hey, Columbo, Prince," he said, greeting the horses standing nearby. "And Princess," he said, turning to Anya. "Hey, have you seen Will?"

Every nerve in Anya's body buzzed up to high alert. Instead of answering him, she glanced around, checking for anyone who might be in hearing distance before whispering, "What did you just say?"

"Oh, right," Josh said. "You hate when I call you that, which is kind of weird because my little sister *makes* me call her Princess."

Anya didn't care about Josh's little sister. Her entire career at Covington was at stake. And she had been so careful! "Who told you?" she demanded. "How did you find out?"

For a moment, Josh said nothing. Anya waited for him to confess that he'd hacked her computer or gone through her belongings in order to discover her secret, but all he finally said was, "Um . . . I can't tell you because I don't know what you're talking about."

Anya didn't believe that for a second. "Every time you see me, you tease me about it!"

"No, not every time —"

"And I can't take it anymore! It's like blackmail!"

At that, Josh took a step back. "Wait, okay, if it's like blackmail, then shouldn't I be getting something for —?"

His babbling made Anya want to scream. "You got me. All right? You win! My dad's the maharaja, which makes *me* the princess!"

Anya had to give Josh credit for faking surprise so well. His eyes bugged, his mouth dropped open, and he made a high piercing noise like "Whaau!" that could have shattered glass. "What?" he managed to say clearly after spluttering a few more non-word sounds of astonishment. "Dude, that is sick! So you're, like, *a princess?*"

Why, oh, why did he keep saying that word? "Shhhh!" Anya ordered, doing her best to shoot daggers out of her eyes.

Josh shushed.

Anya desperately wondered what to do. She liked Josh, she really did, because he was fun to be around and he made her laugh. He had also offered her friendship, and she cherished it. But had he just been acting all nice and sweet, all the while knowing that he could shatter her lifelong dream at any moment? Had he been teasing her all along on purpose? Or was he really so dense that he had never known the truth but had just stumbled upon it? She thought she knew him, but she realized she really didn't. People could surprise you, especially when secrets were involved. She knew that from hard experience.

There was no way around it. She had to take charge and show him who was boss. She had to make him understand that this wasn't a game or a funny joke—it was her life.

She grabbed his arm with both hands. "I don't know how you found out, but I need your silence. I need you to swear on your life." When he only babbled as if he didn't understand, she squeezed, curling her fingers so that they jabbed into his flesh. "Swear!" Yes, she was a princess, but she was a princess who did her own physical work these days, now that she was at Covington. She lugged saddles around and mucked out stalls just like everybody else. She'd built up some pretty impressive muscles and had promised herself to never allow wealth and privilege to make her weak ever again.

Josh hopped in pain, crying out, "Ah! I swear! I swear! I swear on my life!"

She let go. Her fingers ached from gripping so hard, but she had made her point. Josh had sworn himself to secrecy.

"Oww." Josh gently shook his arm out. "Dude, you're as bad as Elaine."

Over by the stable, Kit was snuggling happily against TK's neck when Nav set a stepladder down next to her. "What's that for?" she asked.

Nav replied, "I think you should try."

"Try what?" Kit asked, trying to sound innocent.

"Well, TK was scared, but he found his courage. Can you find yours?"

It was a direct challenge, and Nav was right to make that challenge. Kit knew it was time for her get back on the horse, literally. "Oh," she said, wringing her hands. "Oh, boy. Uh, all right." She gingerly climbed up to the top step as TK stood patiently. He wasn't saddled, so at least there were no stirrups to get caught up in, should she fall. Kit grasped a fistful of his mane with her left hand, put her right hand on his far hip, leaned forward, and jumped . . .

Meanwhile, in the tack room, Will approached Rudy's desk and set down a file. He'd been working extra hard lately, trying to ease his guilt about Rudy's injury. Rudy wasn't aware of just how much he knew about horses and running a stable, and he could take over certain duties to ease Rudy's burden for a while. "These are the vaccination records for stable two," he said.

Rudy glanced up from his paperwork, looking surprised and pleased by Will's efficiency. "Thanks. Good work—" He was interrupted by what sounded like a party outside, especially one particular high-pitched laugh.

"What's that?" Will asked, glancing at the door.

"That," Rudy said, setting down his pen, "is the sound my kid used to make when she was going down the big slide." He struggled to his feet and reached for his cane. "Oh, I've got to see this."

Will helped him hobble to the door. When they got to the outer courtyard, they were greeted by the sight of Nav standing next to TK, while atop the horse, sitting straight and proud—and grinning like a loon—was Kit.

"Unbelievable!" Rudy said. "What a brave kid!"

Kit felt brave, all right, but more than that, she felt complete again. Clever Nav, he must have known that the connection between horse and rider wasn't just a mental thing. It was physical as well. Getting on TK was an accomplishment for her, but doing so *bareback* had been an accomplishment for TK. He had shown none of his usual skittishness but had stood still, as if he'd decided now was the right time to heal their relationship. *Like electricity*, Kit thought, patting TK's neck and feeling the raw energy within him. *You don't get a spark unless both wires come together!*

With a final pat, she slid off TK's back and ran to her dad. She hugged him as he said, "I am so proud of you!"

Kit next hugged a very surprised Nav. "Thank you so much!" she said to him. "I never would have been able to do it without you!"

Nav smiled so hard that he was in danger of damaging his facial muscles. "My pleasure," he gushed. "Truly."

Neither of them noticed Will still standing by the stable door, alone, his expression blank as he took in the scene. He tried not to be jealous of Nav, but he was, and it hurt. He wanted to be the one who helped Kit. He liked her a lot more than he'd thought, a lot more than he should, and it probably wasn't a good thing. All he ever managed to do was get in trouble, while Kit was trying to seriously accomplish something with her life. He grew more and more disappointed with himself as he mulled over those dark thoughts.

Someone took his arm. "I need to talk to you." Rather roughly, Elaine pulled him into the stable.

"Whoa, what do you want?" Will asked, annoyed.

"It was Nav," she declared.

Will blinked. "What? Who told you that?"

"Oh, please. As if I didn't recognize the old *wheel of suspects* routine where one of you blames the next who blames the next until I'm left with twenty suspects instead of one."

Will wasn't in the mood for this. "You're crazy," he said.

She just smirked. "But you made a classic blunder. You forgot to blame the actual culprit. You see, everyone was blamed *except for Nav*."

Will had to admit that Elaine's chain of logic was flawless. She was just basing her logic on the wrong assumptions.

"I'm telling Lady C everything," Elaine finished boldly.

"Oh—" Will said, searching for the right words. If Kit ever found out he was involved in the Guy Fawkes incident, his life would get even darker than it already was. "Oh, you can't do that."

"Oh, I can! I'm just warning you so you can duck."

As Elaine walked away, looking full of misplaced confidence, Will tried to think what to do. All for one and one for all—that was the agreement the Juniper boys had made, but thanks to Elaine, it was falling apart. Should he call the guys together during his work break and arrange a group confession before Elaine told the headmistress? Maybe their punishment would be less harsh if they came forward instead of getting nailed by a third party. But Kit would never forgive him if she found out he was responsible for her dad's injury. If only Elaine would mind her own business!

Irritated, he went back to the tack room, where he found Rudy in high spirits. "Did you see that?" Rudy crowed. "Kit and that horse have come so far so fast!" But then his joy turned to pain as he placed the saddle he was holding on a saddle rack for cleaning. His injured leg buckled, and he almost fell.

"You should really get off that foot for a while," Will advised.

"Ah, I'm too excited. You'll understand when you become a dad. You lose all sense of cool when your kid succeeds."

Great. Fathers and sons. Just one more subject to make Will's heart sink further. "Yeah," he said, and resumed his job cleaning tack.

"What about your folks?" Rudy asked. "Are they coming down for the House Cup? I hear most of them do."

Ah, yes, there it was, the core of that particular set of troubles. Will usually kept mum regarding his family. He didn't like to talk about them. But Rudy had grown on him, almost like a father-away-from-home. "My dad's got a new baby," he found himself saying, brushing the dirt off a riding helmet perhaps a little too hard. "And his wife, the dread Tanya, won't let him go anywhere. Not that he minds."

A moment passed before Rudy asked, "What about your mom?"

"She's in Thailand, I think," Will said, brushing the helmet even harder. "Or Bali. I don't know. I lose track."

"Well, just remember that you'll have your housemates there cheering for you, and at least one equestrian supervisor with no sense of cool." Rudy patted Will on the shoulder.

The touch felt like a father's touch. It made all the emotions churning around in Will's chest flare up like evil firecrackers—longing, loneliness, frustration, rejection, and guilt, lots and lots of guilt. He felt guilt for disappointing his father, though he didn't even know how he might have done that, and guilt for making his mother want to leave the family *and* the country, though he didn't know how he'd done that, either, and on top of all that, guilt for having injured the equestrian supervisor, who was the first man who had ever shown an interest in him as a person rather than seeing him as a burden. Will thought he might explode.

He shot to his feet. "I have something to tell you."

Rudy turned around.

"I'm the one who did it." The words felt like ashes in Will's mouth. "I caused the whole thing. I didn't think anything bad would happen. We just wanted to win. I didn't think it through." He cringed, figuring that Rudy would get angry. He was right.

"You don't mess with the horses' living environment!" Rudy yelled, looking shocked by the admission. "They're stuck—they can't run!"

"I know! It was really stupid, I get that now, and I'm sorry!" Will waited to get chewed out more, but Rudy just turned his back on him. That was it, then. Will and Rudy had had something good going. Now it was gone, and it was his own fault. "You must really hate me," Will said.

"No," Rudy replied, drawing out the word so that it sounded like a sigh. "It takes character to admit when you've done something wrong."

"It would have been better to just not do it in the first place."

"Yeah, and it would be better if I won the lottery and didn't have to dig out a stall for the rest of my life, but that's not the world we're living in, is it?"

Nearby, in TK's stall, Kit was beside herself with joy. "My big, brave handsome boy, I am so super-mega-crazy proud of you!"

TK tossed his head and whinnied as if in agreement.

"Oh," Kit said. "And so modest." She exited the stall and closed the door. "Now, you get all your beauty sleep, because there are more fun times to be had tomorrow."

Head toss, whinny, grunt, grunt, whuffle!

Kit laughed, imagining that TK wasn't just looking forward to tomorrow. He had definite plans of his own for fun times, and she couldn't wait! As she hung his lead rope on a hook, she heard a voice from the tack room. It was Will. "I know, I know—I have to tell Lady Covington."

Then her dad said, "Well, no one else can do it for you."

Curious, Kit opened the tack room door and peeked inside. She saw her father sitting on the edge of his desk, arms folded. He did not look happy as Will's voice continued: "So I just go in and say, 'All right, Lady Covington! I'm the one who stole all the Guys and hid them in the ceiling, so I'm responsible for Mr. Bridges's accident and for spooking all of the horses and everything and—'" He stopped when Kit opened the door all the way. "Kit . . ."

She couldn't believe what she'd just heard. Will? All along it had been *Will*? "How could you do this?" she cried, and fled the room.

Chapter 6

PAINFUL TRUTHS

This is so wrong! Kit thought in a daze, passing stall after stall, walking as fast as she could with no idea where she was going. She didn't care, as long as it was away from Will Palmerston. Of all the people to pull such a horrible stunt, *he* was the one? And all this time, he had hidden it from her, during all those hours that night with her at the hospital, all the classes they'd had together since then, all the meals they had shared, and all the times when they'd just smiled at each other as they'd passed in the hallways? She was so angry! *No, that's not a strong enough word,* she thought. *I'm furious! I'm enraged!*

"Kit!" Will yelled from behind her. "Kit, stop! Please! It was an accident!"

Accident? The word made her whirl around, fists balled. "Oh, so you *accidentally* stole every other house's Guy?"

Will caught up with her. "No, I guess not," he admitted.

"So the *accident* part was when you *accidentally* hid them in an incredibly dangerous place with the horses?"

"I know!" Will said. "It was a really big mistake!"

Kit saw the pain and guilt in his eyes and tried to calm down. At least he knew what a stupendous jerk he'd been. But she deserved to have her say. "Everyone makes mistakes—I get that. I really do."

That surprised him. "Yeah?"

"But you didn't make a mistake," she went on. "A mistake is forgetting your textbook or setting your hair on fire in eighth-grade science."

Will paused. "That happened?"

So not what she wanted to explain. "It was a Thursday, third period. David Kempton laughed so hard, he fell off his stool. But the point is, I didn't hurt another person or an animal!"

"I didn't know all that would happen—"

Kit didn't let him finish. He wasn't allowed to defend himself. This was her rightful chance to react to the full scope of what he had done, and he was going to listen. "What were you even thinking?" she demanded. "The horses could have been hurt, too!"

"I know—"

"Like, *seriously* hurt! What if it was Wayne? Or Prince? Or any of them?"

"I didn't know the roof would cave in. I didn't think."

And now came the core of it all. She had to say it out loud, as if to purge her heart of all the fear and worry that she'd been carrying around since that fateful bonfire night. "TK is afraid again. Of everything! And my dad's foot got *fractured*. They're all I've got!" That made her cringe. How had her life gotten so small that her "family" consisted of one man and a horse? And the mother she no longer had . . . "I can't just pretend that this didn't happen," she finished quietly. *There. I said it*, she thought. *Now please apologize, Will. Apologize and end this mess, okay?*

Will's jaw clenched. He stared off to one side, unable to face her.

Please, Will. I can't do it. You have to. Say you're sorry so we can start over again. Show me that our friendship is strong enough to handle this, please! I need you to do this for me!

Will remained silent.

The moment passed.

"Right." Tears stung at Kit's eyes, but she refused to let them fall. Quite the contrary—she stood straighter, set her shoulders back, and said, "See you around." She forced herself to turn and leave with controlled, purposeful strides.

She didn't hear Will say softly, only after she was gone, "I'm sorry."

Nav showed up, dressed for his afternoon ride on Prince. "Hey, Will," he said. Then, seeing Will's expression, he asked, "Everything okay?"

"Just back off," Will snarled, walking away.

"If you need to kick some walls," Nav called after him, "do it on your side of the room!"

Wednesday came around, and Kit found herself at another afternoon tea in Lady Covington's spotless office.

By now Kit knew the drill: how to dress properly, how to act, and what things to compliment, such as the beautiful fern that the headmistress grew by the window or the lovely quality of the tea (which she couldn't actually taste, but that didn't matter—the compliment did). "These tiny sandwiches are just delicious, Lady Covington," she said super politely.

The headmistress nodded to acknowledge Kit's manners, but she said, "I didn't invite you to tea to discuss sandwiches. Their size, their taste, or anything else for that matter."

Of course not, Kit thought. There was only one thing on Lady Covington's mind, so Kit came right out with it. "I'm happy to report that I did, in fact, ride TK."

"Sitting on top of an animal to pose for a photograph does not a rider make. Do you imagine that every child who has ever sat on a pony at a birthday party is a rider? Everyone who has perched atop an elephant or a camel at the zoo?"

Kit knew Lady Covington better these days, so she was ready for such a remark. "I actually trotted around the ring on him," she stated proudly.

"But according to the schedule," said Lady Covington, pronouncing it *shedyool*, as the English did, "you should be way beyond that. Where is the problem? With you? With the horse? With your equestrian tutor?"

Kit struggled to maintain her new sense of proper behavior. Lady Covington had just handed her a perfect opportunity to bad-mouth Elaine! But the fact was: "Elaine's a good teacher." It was the truth. And it was only right for her to continue with another truth: "TK and I are just kind of on our own sked."

Lady Covington graced Kit with a tight smile. "Congratulations! I didn't realize that you and TK had been appointed headmistress of this institution."

That much raw sarcasm knocked the wind right out of Kit's sails. What could she say to that?

Lady Covington remained unrelenting. "You will ride in the House Cup."

Kit almost choked on her tea. "What? But that's a huge deal! Everybody's already talking about it.

Elaine's made stat sheets! I can't see how TK and I are going to be ready to compete."

"Well, *get* ready. This is an official show. It will greatly impact your BSEA standing."

With so many clubs and leagues and associations in England's world of competitive horsemanship, Kit still couldn't get all the names straight. Her confusion must have shown on her face.

"The British Schools Equestrian Association," explained Lady Covington patiently, "and yes, it is quite as important as it sounds."

"Oh. Right."

"You wouldn't want to let your housemates down, would you? If you fail, Rose Cottage will lose the cup." She paused long enough that Kit opened her mouth to start flailing out an excuse. "And as you know," the headmistress continued, neatly cutting Kit off, "U.K. Boarding School of the Year is our goal. This will help get us there. But if you can't meet this goal, TK will have to go. It doesn't make sense to keep a horse that can't compete."

Kit couldn't have sipped any more tea if she wanted to. Her throat was squeezing itself shut. No matter how many times she had heard this threat and managed to overcome it, this was her last chance with TK. She could feel it. Lady Covington had had enough, and if Kit and TK did not perform well in the House Cup, Kit would lose him. End of subject.

Lady Covington was not totally heartless, however. She gave Kit a smile. "Have a lovely afternoon," she said.

Yeah, right. Slurp some tea, munch some tiny sandwiches, and oh, by the way, you have to do the impossible or your life will spin down the drain. Kit tried to smile back as she said, "Yes, Lady Covington." She stood and headed for the door.

Lady Covington wasn't finished. "Don't forget your bag. You might need it later if you get hungry."

"Oh, yeah. For sure." Kit grabbed her leather tassel purse, then stopped. She got that sinking feeling she got whenever her dad caught her doing something sneaky. "Wait, how did you . . . ?"

Lady Covington turned away. "Good afternoon."

Busted, Kit thought as she closed the door behind her. *So why did she let me get away with snagging those treats? She's so confusing!* When she turned around to head for the main corridor, she met yet another confusing sight: Will. He was apparently waiting to see the headmistress.

Their eyes locked.

Will broke the stare first.

Reining in her disappointment, Kit hurried on her way. As she headed for the student lounge, she made a decision. *I am going to stay cheerful,* she thought. *Even if it kills me. I will not let Lady C get me down. TK and I will work hard to be ready for the cup, we will do a spectacular job, and everything will turn out sunny-side up. I will not accept any other outcome, so there!* She imagined herself sticking her tongue out at the headmistress — not disrespectfully, but in a playful manner, like she did with her dad. It was her way of saying, "I accept your challenge, so look out!"

Feeling better, she opened the heavy oak door of the student lounge. "I don't know how Lady C does it," she said, grabbing a chair and plopping down at the table where Anya, Elaine, and Peaches were studying together. "I waited until she excused herself," she went on, pulling a bundle wrapped in a cloth napkin from her bag, "but she still somehow busted me on making a doggie bag." Kit unwrapped the bundle, presenting a pile of pilfered tea munchies to the girls. "The scones are to die for."

She expected them to ooh and aah over the booty and dive in, but Anya and Peaches glanced at Elaine first as if waiting for some kind of permission. *Oh, good grief,* Kit thought.

As if Elaine had heard the thought, she glowered at Kit. "It's *scone.* Pronounced like *gone.* Which you should be after stealing all that."

Kit shrugged. "Don't eat it if you don't like it. But you-snooze-you-lose on the chocolate shortbread, lady. I had to sit through a boring hour of *blah, blah, blah*! I've earned it."

As if that signaled a green light, Anya hungrily took a piece of shortbread. Elaine, however, defended tradition by stating, "Tea with the headmistress is a *privilege.*"

Kit was ready to quip, "It's a snore fest," when Anya asked her, "What did you talk about all alone with Lady C? World events? Languages? Oh, I know—history!"

"What?" Kit laughed. "Nah. I blabbed on about how to break your jeans down to the perfect shade of worn. Eventually Lady C fell into a deep sleep, so I drew a mustache on her face with a marker and jumped out the window!" *If only,* she thought.

Anya's eyes grew big and round. She almost dropped her shortbread.

"I'm kidding," Kit told her before her naive roomie had a heart attack. "We talked about—what else? Me riding TK." Her voice dipped at that last part. *No! Do not let it get to you! Stay light and peppy, light and peppy!*

Anya unsuccessfully hid a wicked grin behind her hand. "Is it wrong that I secretly wish you'd done the mustache thing?"

"If it's wrong, I don't want to be right!" Kit said. *Okay, I might as well get it over with. Remember, light and peppy.* "Oh, and Elaine?" she added. "I'm apparently competing in the cup."

Elaine's pale skin grew a shade paler. "You've got to be joking."

"You wish." *I wish. The whole school is going to wish! But I'm not joking.* Kit mentally gritted her teeth. *Keep up the light and peppy—don't lose it now!* "Toss me a tart," she said brightly to Anya. She expected more snark from Miss Perfect, but Elaine suddenly jumped tracks.

"You know, Kit," she said in a helpful tone, "it would be rude not to invite Lady Covington to a reciprocal tea. You really must."

Kit studied Elaine's face. Was she serious? Kit had never heard of students inviting the headmistress to tea, but maybe it was one of those weird English etiquette things she hadn't heard about yet. Feeling lost, she turned to Anya for guidance.

Startled, Anya's eyes darted from Elaine to Kit, back to Elaine, and then back to Kit. "Oh! Uh, it's quite definitely the proper thing to do," she finally told Kit.

"Okay," Kit said with a shrug. "I'll text her."

Kit could almost feel the jealousy radiate from Elaine in hot waves. "Wait—you've got Lady Covington's *phone number?*"

Kit grinned. "No. But I have a sense of humor."

Elaine slowly got up and collected her things. "Or you could send her a proper handwritten invitation," she suggested. "From Rose Cottage as a whole."

Kit liked that idea. The more, the merrier! Anything positive to take her mind off Lady C's threat and Will's guilt and her own anger and—*Oh, why did you have to think of that? Stop it! Pull yourself together!* "All right," she told Elaine. "Cool! Yeah, let's do that!"

If only Kit knew what happened once Elaine and Peaches left the room.

"I'm a titch confused," Peaches said. "Why are you helping Kit?"

"I've got goals," replied Elaine. "I deserve access. Why isn't Lady Covington taking a special interest in *me* and *my* riding?"

Peaches paused. "How do you want me to answer that?"

Elaine faced her henchwoman straight on. "If Kit gets special treatment, *I'm* going to use it as an opportunity."

Chapter 7

MESSAGES RECEIVED

Josh barged into Will and Nav's dorm room. "Have you seen Will?"

Nav was lounging in a deep leather reclining chair that was so polished it gleamed like glass. His legs were up, and an open textbook was in his hands. "Not today," he said. "He was up and out the door before morning bells."

Josh made a point of shutting the door behind him and then stepped over a pile of clothes on the floor. As usual, Will's belongings lay strewn haphazardly all over his side of the room, while Nav sat in spotless splendor in his half of the room. "Dude, he *confessed*! To the Guy crime thing!" As if the weight of the news had worn him out, Josh sank down on the messy unmade bed. "He went right to Lady C, and right to her face, dude, he just totally told her! To her face!"

Nav snapped his book shut. "Why would he do that? We said we'd all take responsibility!"

"It's like she controlled his thoughts. She's like twelve evil masterminds all rolled up into one terrifying lady package!"

Nav shook his head. "He must have gotten caught somehow."

"Pixie told Winston, who told Cooper, who told Anya, who told me," Josh said. "Will got a ton of extra duties."

"Oh," said Nav thoughtfully. "I bet I know why he confessed." He got up from the recliner, removed the pair of satin slippers from his feet, and grabbed his riding jacket from its hook by his dresser.

"Dude, is this room, like, twice as big as the rest of them?" Josh asked, but Nav just strode past and left, slamming the door.

Josh stood alone. "It is *nice* in here," he said. He put on Nav's comfy slippers and decided to take a test nap in the reclining chair.

Kit finished tacking up TK for a ride, which hadn't been easy. Will had offered to help, but she was still so angry with him that she'd flatly refused. This had resulted in him barking things like, "Better tighten that girth!" and "Noseband's crooked!" and "Stirrups look too short!" every time he walked by, which he did way too often considering he was supposed to be mucking out stalls. She was grateful when Nav showed up.

"Katarina," he greeted her, using the nickname he had apparently just bestowed upon her. "Great to see you. Are you going for a ride? Prince and I would be happy to join you."

"I wish," Kit said, "but I have another inspiring training session with Elaine."

"Perhaps we could ask Lady Covington if I could step in for Elaine," Nav suggested.

Kit felt a stirring of hope. "Do you think she'd go for that?"

Will strode past, a shovel angled over his shoulder. "Not a chance," he commented, disappearing around the corner.

Kit frowned as Nav said, "He may be right, but that doesn't mean you and I can't go for a ride sometime."

"Not without a chaperone!" came Will's voice two stalls down.

Kit ignored it. "That sounds great," she told Nav, "but right now, I've got to go."

Nav nodded. "Let's be sure to arrange a ride together soon."

Kit watched him go, patting TK's neck. Maybe Nav was her secret note writer, she thought. He was always trying to help her, so it only made sense. It was kind of cute how he pretended to know nothing about it, and yet just now he'd called her *Katarina* with that amazing accent of his. How romantic!

Maybe he had a crush on her. She grinned.

A half hour later, out in the practice ring, Kit guided TK in a big figure eight while Elaine trotted next to her on Thunder.

Kit had to struggle to keep TK calm because her own mind was buzzing with way too many thoughts: Nav's riding invitation, her dad's foot, the House Cup competition, Lady C's threat, her math homework, the itch on her left big toe that she wouldn't be able to scratch for at least another half hour, and last but hardly least, the Rose Cottage tea she was planning for Lady Covington. She wanted to tell Elaine about her ideas, but she wanted to pick the right moment.

TK made it back to the start of the figure eight, so Kit gently pulled him to a stop.

"That was a reasonable attempt," said Elaine.

"Whoa," Kit responded with a teasing smile. "*Reasonable* from you? That's like a triple A plus!"

As usual, Elaine ignored the compliment. "Do not lean," she snapped.

Kit sat up straighter.

"But do not be inflexible, either."

"That's an interesting note, coming from you."

"What does that mean?" Elaine said defensively. "I'm flexible."

Talk about a perfect opening! Kit leaped for it, talking quickly to get it all out before Elaine could interrupt. "Oh, good! Because I'm really excited about this brainstorm I had. For the Lady C tea? I'm hoping you'll be on board with it. I want to do it back-home style, so the cook's ordering beef for sliders and a ton of lemons for the Arnold Palmers!"

The blank expression on Elaine's face was priceless. "Okay, look," she said. "You're going to have to stop speaking gibberish if we're going to communicate."

"Mini hamburgers," Kit explained, "and lemon-ade mixed with iced tea! I want to show Lady C that tea doesn't have to be stuffy." She knew the idea was pretty far out, but mini hamburgers had to be accept-able, right? Because Lady C's teas always had mini sandwiches. Mini was mini, wasn't it? And Arnold Palmers included iced tea, so the tea was there, just cold instead of hot. And mixed with something else. But it was there. It wasn't like she wanted to serve something totally left field like diet soda and buffalo wings.

Elaine looked like she was going to faint. She dismounted Thunder, seemed to gather herself for a moment, and then said, "Lady Covington's tea with Rose Cottage is not going to be a hoedown. Beef burgers? Cold drinks? What's next, banana splits?"

Kit clapped her hands in delight. "That's a great idea!" *Why didn't I think of that?*

"*No,*" Elaine declared. "No, it is a terrible idea! Clotted cream, finger sandwiches, and *hot tea.* That is a proper English tea. That is what one serves to a headmistress."

"A little change never hurt anyone," Kit said, annoyed now. What was it about being *proper* that had so many English people caught in such a spell? It was like saying that chocolate could only be served on a white plate in one-inch cubes. Sure, it was yummy that way, but what about chocolate candy bars? And Fudgsicles? And Black Forest cake? None of those would exist if people only ate chocolate on white plates in one-inch cubes!

"Maybe you're right," Elaine murmured thoughtfully. "Maybe change is just what we need. . . ."

Will liked working in the stables. Unlike most other Covington students, he enjoyed hard physical labor, and he liked getting to know all the horses, most of which he considered better friends than many of his human acquaintances. Animals made sense to him. Their communications were honest, their needs simple, and their affections uncomplicated. People were so much harder to deal with on all counts.

Today's case in point: Sally Warrington and her latest food delivery to a certain injured equestrian supervisor.

Will stayed quietly in the corner of the tack room, pretending to sweep, as Sally tiptoed in and set a cake on Rudy's desk. As with all the so-called "food" that Sally had made thus far, the cake appeared questionable: dark chocolate frosting with . . . melon slices on top?

He melted farther into the corner when Rudy limped in, using his cane. He seemed to hate that cane. It always put him in a lousy mood.

"Miss Sally," Rudy said when he saw her.

Will liked the way he called her Miss Sally. It sounded so authentically cowboyish.

"Oh!" said Sally, startled. "Hello! Um, I thought I might just bring you a little treat." She gestured to her cake, clearly pleased with herself.

Will winced. This wasn't going to end the way Sally wanted.

Sure enough, grumpy Rudy said, "I don't need"—he eyed the bizarre cake—"anything. Thanks."

"Oh. Right, then." Poor Sally began to stutter in embarrassment. "Should I—? Do you want me to—? Shall I—?"

"Leave it there, please," Rudy instructed. "And

do not bring me another one." At her hurt look, he added, "I'm not helpless. I can eat in the dining hall like everyone else."

Will knew how Sally felt. Rejected. He could see it in the way her bright expression slowly crumbled. "Message received," she said. "Good day, Mr. Bridges." She wasted no time getting out of there.

Will let out the breath he'd been holding. Sally Warrington was a sweet lady, and Rudy had given her the verbal equivalent of a slap. "That was a bit harsh," he commented.

"You want to try the cake?" Rudy barked. "'Cause we both know it's going to taste like hay."

Oh, yes, he was crabby, all right. "She was trying to help," Will said.

"Do I look like I need help?"

"Honestly? A little bit." Rudy glared at him, but Will pressed on. "Point is, I think she fancies you."

Rudy took that idea with a surprised look. "Fancies me?"

"Yeah. Or, I don't know, she just feels really bad about what happened. Everybody does." Considering it had been his fault, Will felt a bit bold saying those words to a teacher, but it was the truth.

Rudy changed the subject. "I got a note from Lady Covington telling me I'm not allowed to have you on horseback except in class."

Will resumed sweeping. "Yeah. Apparently."

"Do you want to talk about that? That's a lot of punishment for one person. . . ."

"No." That was the last thing Will wanted. Why waste time talking about something that couldn't be changed?

The tack room descended into silence as instructor and student focused on their work.

A couple days later, Kit was on her way back to her dorm room, having just taken a shower, when she saw Peaches emerge from her room next door. She was fully dressed in her uniform with her brown hair styled in simple loose curls, and she was clutching a yellow envelope carefully in both hands.

"Hey, Peaches," Kit said. "What are you doing up so early? Did Elaine pour cold water on your head?"

"Practically," Peaches replied. "She set my alarm for me and then totally hauled me out of bed because—" She cut herself off with a chipmunk squeak, jamming the yellow envelope inside her jacket as if Kit hadn't obviously seen it already. "Um, nothing! Bye!" She scurried past Kit and around the corner.

What the heck was that about? Kit wondered, gazing after her. *Is Elaine up to something?* She decided to find out.

It wasn't long before she and Anya were dressed and making their way to Lady Covington's office. "But why there?" Anya asked when Kit revealed their destination.

"Because Peaches was definitely on a secret mission for Elaine," Kit explained. "Plus, that yellow envelope smelled like flowers, and Lady C always sends messages and invitations on smelly flower paper. Elaine would totally do the same for her." Kit knew that because the flower scent had been the reason TK had eaten her first invitation to tea with the headmistress weeks ago. "I'm betting that whatever that note is, Peaches delivered it here," she finished as they reached Lady Covington's office.

Kit had already established that Lady Covington was elsewhere, so she knew the office would be empty. She and Anya slipped inside as Anya whispered, "Can I just be the lookout? I'm shaking! Surely that's a bad quality in a spy!"

Poor Anya, Kit thought. *She must have lived her whole childhood without ever sneaking away from her babysitter or setting booby traps for her dad or stealing freshly baked cookies from under her mom's nose.* She grasped her friend by the shoulders and said encouragingly, "Embrace the fear."

Anya moaned.

Kit headed straight for the headmistress's desk. Before she even got there, she spotted the bright-yellow envelope sitting on top of a stack of mail. "I knew it!" she whispered to Anya, picking it up and taking the note out. She read over it quickly. "Elaine changed everything, including the time and the place of the tea. She's trying to cut us out!"

"It's today at four p.m.?" Anya said as she looked at the invitation. "We'll never make that!"

Both girls looked up at the sound of a voice outside: "This afternoon? No, I'm sorry—I believe I'm previously engaged. Let me just check, and I'll give you a ring." The doorknob rattled.

Kit and Anya gaped at each other. Lady Covington was back!

As the door swung open, they did the only thing they could—they dived underneath the desk and watched as Lady Covington's feet walked toward them. As she headed for one side of the desk, they squished more toward each other. Anya gestured in silent terror to Kit's foot that was sticking out too far. Kit pulled it back in, trying to force her leg to bend in ways that Mother Nature hadn't intended. As she winced in pain, she noticed that Anya's hand was about to get squashed by a sensible black pump. She pointed wildly, and Anya snatched her hand back just in time, stifling a giggle. Kit glared at her, but Anya just shrugged back helplessly.

Lady Covington mumbled, "Oh, dear, what did I do with it?" as the girls heard the shuffling of papers on the desk. "Hm, I thought it was . . ." The headmistress's feet stepped to the side of the desk, her right foot so close to Kit that Kit could almost see her reflection in the shoe's shiny surface.

Suddenly Kit realized what Lady Covington was looking for—the tea invitation that was currently in her own hand! She flapped it at Anya, whose jaw dropped in horror. Before she could analyze just how risky the move would be, Kit slid the invitation right under Lady Covington's toes.

"What on earth . . . ?" The headmistress must have glanced down, because the girls heard a chuckle. "Oh, dear!" A hand appeared and picked up the invitation. "Ah, yes." Lady Covington's feet then moved over to a table where a phone was located. With her back now to her desk, she began to punch in a number.

This was the only chance the girls were going to get. Kit poked Anya, and they both silently scrambled out from under the desk. They backed their way to the door, hoping like mad that Lady Covington wouldn't turn around. If she did . . . well, Kit didn't want to go there. Anya managed to open the door without a sound, and they both slipped out as the headmistress said to her caller, "Hello? Yes, I did just check my calendar, and I am engaged this afternoon. Next week?"

Kit shut the door behind them, and Anya released a giggle. "Sorry. I always get the giggles in the face of impending doom!"

"So doesn't matter," said Kit. "We got it!"

Anya grimaced. "Where does she find those shoes, though? Hideous! I'll send her some links. Anonymously, of course."

The door opened, and Lady Covington smiled at them. It wasn't a totally friendly smile. They were, after all, loitering in her waiting area. "I thought I heard tittering," she said.

"Lady Covington," Kit began, then just hung there, wondering what to say. She had to say something! "After, um, studying the weather patterns—"

"It seems that rain is in the forecast," Anya piped up.

Kit nudged her as if to say, "Way to go!" She picked up the story with, "We were wondering if you could meet in the dining hall."

"Would the time remain the same?" Lady Covington asked, suspicion flashing across her face. It didn't bother Kit. She figured it was the headmistress's job to look suspicious.

"Could we meet a little earlier?" Anya asked. "Three thirty instead of four?"

Anya, Kit thought, *you are brilliant!* She decided to make the request more vital by saying, "I have a riding engagement scheduled at five, which I know you wouldn't want me to miss."

Lady Covington, arms crossed with one finger tapping thoughtfully, finally nodded. "I'd be delighted."

"Our pleasure," said Anya.

Kit was so relieved that she blurted out, "So much delight . . . in—in all the pleasure of—of . . ."

Lady Covington pointed to the hallway. "Off you go."

The girls turned obediently and marched away, huddled together and hardly believing their luck. They'd done it! They'd outsmarted Elaine! Once out of the headmistress's sight, they high-fived each other and began to run.

Chapter 8

APOLOGIES AND RIVALRIES

In the tack room, Rudy sat at his desk going over the objectives for his next riding class when Nav appeared in the doorway. "What can I do for you, Mr. Andrada?"

"Sir." Nav entered, shoving his hands into his pockets. "I wanted to ask if I could take another student out for a hack. Um . . . Katherine, actually."

Curious, Rudy pushed his papers aside to indicate that Nav should continue. He sensed that the boy was going to explode if he didn't speak.

"Her riding has improved greatly," Nav said, "and I'm guessing that she could take a break from Elaine." That last part was said with a forced chuckle.

Rudy sensed an ulterior motive and casually leaned forward. "And you're doing this just out of the goodness of your heart?" he asked.

Nav was caught off guard. "Sir?"

"Did you hear about Will's punishment?"

"I did not."

"Poor kid's only allowed to ride in class. Indefinitely."

Nav glanced at the floor. Rudy could practically feel the guilt roiling around him, and he knew why. "Thing is, son, you and I both know he didn't pull that stunt off all by himself. But he took responsibility for it. He took the heat so the rest of you wouldn't have to. Now, I would think that trying to help your buddy out might be your biggest concern at the moment."

Rudy felt like a teenager again as he sensed Nav's inner turmoil—shock that his real motives had been discovered, guilt about Will's fate, embarrassment that he had tried to take advantage of it, and confusion about what to say next. Nav finally just spun on his heels and left.

Rudy tried not to feel too bad about putting Nav on the spot like that. Being a teenager could be so hard. He'd been a real handful of trouble himself when he'd been young. He often wondered how the adults in his past had ever managed to mold him into the dependable, respectable adult that he was now.

"Dependable?" he questioned himself. "Eh. Maybe a little. Respectable?" He snorted and resumed his paperwork.

Will had put on the janitor's coveralls about ten minutes ago, and he loathed them already. They made him feel old and tired and boxed in by rotten circumstances. Mucking out stalls was one thing. Mucking out classrooms was quite another. It was an insult, that's what it was.

Today's extra punishment was to clean this entire staircase and the upper floor. That meant sweeping and vacuuming and mopping and, the worst part, polishing. He parked the yellow janitor's cart at the base of the staircase and sighed. There was nothing he could do but get started.

Nav trotted down the stairs.

"Oh, what?" Will snarled at him. "You going to stomp up and down in your boots to make sure all the steps are as dirty as possible?"

More boys appeared. Juniper Cottage boys. Josh and Leo and Alex and Wyatt. "You didn't do the crime yourself," Nav said as they all trooped down to Will, "so you shouldn't have to do the time alone, either."

"Yeah, dude," said Josh. "We totally would have gone in with you to take responsibility. I mean, I'm waaay glad I didn't have to. But thank you."

Alex had already grabbed a mop, while Leo had chosen the feather duster. Wyatt took a pump sprayer of glass cleaner and a roll of paper towels. That left a broom for Josh. As for Nav, he waited until the others had trudged upstairs before addressing Will again. "Listen, I'm sorry about before. In the barn?"

"I don't know what you're talking about," said Will, though he knew exactly what Nav was talking about—that time days ago when Nav had asked Kit to take a ride with him, knowing that Will was up to his earlobes in chores.

"Well, anyway," Nav said as he picked up a broom, "all for one!"

Will was now left with the dreaded polish. He smiled. It could have turned out worse.

Elaine was determined to make the Rose Cottage tea with Lady Covington a grand event. She chose a cozy yet elegantly landscaped patch of lawn with a tall hedge along one side and stone pathways on the other sides. Her team of helpers set up four tables draped in crisp white cloths and topped with pots of flowers. Elaine herself hung strings of colorful bunting from poles to add to the gaiety. Most important, only *traditional* English finger sandwiches, pastries, and tea were tastefully arranged on the serving table.

"We have half an hour, people," Elaine announced, clapping her hands. "Tablecloths, napkins, tea, spit spot!"

At the same time in the dining room, Kit was at the helm arranging her barbecue-style Rose Cottage tea. Classic American red-and-white-checked cloths covered each table, along with little vases bursting with big bright marigolds. The serving table was loaded with bowls of potato chips and potato salad, plates of pickle slices, pitchers of premixed Arnold Palmers, and plastic plates, napkins, and utensils.

"This is awesome!" Kit said, encouraging her helpers. "You're like a party-planning army!" She gave Anya, who was checking that all the plastic-ware was arranged properly by each plate, a double thumbs-up.

Rudy was there, too, cooking sliders on two por-table grill presses. Kit was tickled to see him wearing the cook's apron she'd found for him. He had com-plained that it made him look like a greasy-spoon short-order cook, to which she had replied, "Yeah, but you're *my* greasy-spoon short-order cook!" That had made him laugh.

Right now Rudy wasn't laughing, though; he was watching Miss Sally. She stood in the doorway observ-ing the hustle and bustle of tea preparations before she noticed him. He waved his cooking tongs at her and dared a smile, knowing that she might still be upset with him. To her credit, she ambled over. "Did you know I make a mean burger?" he asked.

"Hm, that's fascinating," Sally responded. "And what would be required to make a nice one?"

Ouch. Rudy knew he deserved that, so he took it with grace. "It's really all in the seasoning." He felt awkward now, and realized in alarm that it was the same way he used to feel back when he was a teenager, all nervous and sweaty—about a girl! Oh, for cryin' out loud. *Pull it together, Bridges,* he thought. "Another thing you may not know is that I get really grouchy when I'm hurt," he confessed, some of his nerves calming at the sight of the little grin forming on Sally's lips. "And then when people try to help me, I just . . ." He made a gesture to imply his head exploding. "I don't . . ." He picked up his cane and gave it a shake, irritated. "I don't like feeling helpless."

"Ah. Is that a cowboy thing?"

"No, uh, that's a jerk thing." Rudy was pleased when Sally laughed. "But I will tell you the cowboy way of making it up to a lady. You make her a nice meal."

"Fascinating," said Sally. "And when would you typically offer a lady that sort of meal?"

"Around seven thirty?" Rudy suggested. "Maybe here in the dining hall?"

Sally's grin widened.

Rudy grinned, too. Score!

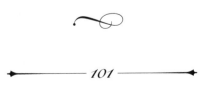

Kit was busy keeping a lookout for Lady Covington, who suddenly appeared at the door. Kit checked her watch—*spot on time*, as the British said.

"Lady Covington!" Kit called. "Welcome!"

The headmistress surveyed the room in dismay. "What in the world . . . ?"

Kit wasn't at all upset by the response. She knew Lady Covington well enough at this point to guess that an indoor picnic would surprise her. *But surprises are good!* she thought. *Sometimes you just have to shake things up.*

Kit took the headmistress's arm. "Your seat," she said, "is right over here." She guided the guest of honor to the head of the first table. The headmistress sat, barely holding back a freak-out as she saw the contents of the plastic plate before her. Kit totally enjoyed her reaction and barreled onward. "Welcome to our down-home barbecue! There's potato salad and sliders!" She lifted one of the bun tops to show the meat patty beneath.

The headmistress's dismay jumped to disgust. "Perhaps they could slide right off my plate."

"Yeah," Kit agreed, "and into your belly!" Refusing to dim her enthusiasm, she held up a pitcher. "And this is my specialty to wash them down." She poured a cup for her guest. "Iced tea with a splash of lemonade!"

Lady Covington eyed the cup as if it might bite. "How many times must I explain to you that you're not back home but rather at an elite British institution that thrives on tradition?"

Yeah, yeah, blah, blah, blah. "Lady Covington, I—"

"Tea is a very serious affair. One expects certain things. *Hot* tea, for instance. Scones." Lady Covington said *scone* so that it rhymed with *gone,* just as Elaine had implored Kit that it should. She went on: "Finger sandwiches—"

Kit dared to interrupt her. "Well, I thought you might say something like that, so I do have some on standby." As planned, Anya was there to hand Kit a more traditional tea serving dish upon which sat a pile of proper finger sandwiches, all with the crusts properly sliced off. "PB&J was my mom's favorite. She used to make these for me on special occasions, and I thought today was special." Kit watched as the headmistress struggled to hold back another complaint. *You can't say it, can you?* Kit thought triumphantly. *See? I listened! I paid attention to the rules! I can honor tradition, too—I just do it my own way!*

With a halfhearted smile, Lady Covington reached for a sandwich, hesitated as if it might be radioactive, then finally picked it up. She nibbled at the edge.

Kit was rewarded by the tiniest smile on Lady Covington's face. *She likes it! She won't say so, but she likes it! Woo, gotcha!* She couldn't stop herself from saying, "*Please* try the iced tea. You might be pleasantly surprised."

"Let's not get carried away," said the headmistress, her words so heavy with sarcasm they could have sunk to the bottom of the ocean.

That didn't faze Kit one bit. She signaled Anya, who whipped out her phone and angled herself to take a photo. Kit leaned down next to Lady Covington and plastered a full-toothed grin on her face as Lady Covington turned to Anya in shock.

Click!

The moment was captured for all to see. In this case, "all" meant Elaine.

Out on the school grounds, in the quiet garden section prepped for a traditional English teatime, Elaine paced anxiously. "It's not like Lady Covington to be late," she said. She pointed at one of her minions. "You! Go check her office."

The minion took off.

Elaine pulled her mobile from her pocket to check if she might have received any messages explaining this unusual circumstance. What she saw was her guest of honor at a completely different tea! And beside her, grinning like the Cheshire cat, was Kit Bridges.

"She won't get away with this," Elaine hissed, and she marched straight for the dining hall.

Chapter 9

SNEAKY, SNEAKY!

Sixteen, fifteen, fourteen, thirteen . . .

Kit waited by the door, counting down from one hundred because that seemed about the right amount of travel time for someone walking very, very fast from the gardens to the dining hall.

Eight, seven, six, five . . .

Yup, she could hear footsteps approaching. Very fast footsteps!

Three, two, one, and —

"I saw your text," Elaine snapped, entering the room and zeroing in on Kit. "How dare you try to sabotage my tea?"

Kit played it as smooth as satin. "You suggested that I invite Lady Covington to tea, and I did. Where's the sabotage, Elaine?"

"When you insisted on making it some kind of rodeo spectacle, I had no choice but to—" She cut herself off before admitting to any misconduct.

"Yes, Elaine?" Kit prompted. This was so much fun! Lady Covington was still sitting at the head table no more than ten feet away! She was listening to the whole conversation, and Elaine had stormed in so quickly that she hadn't taken stock of Lady C's proximity!

Lady Covington couldn't allow the argument to escalate, however. "Elaine?" she called out pleasantly.

Kit enjoyed watching Elaine's face go white as she recognized the voice.

"Nice of you to join us," the headmistress continued. "Would you care for a"—she struggled to remember the word—"slipper?"

"Slider," Kit said gently.

Lady Covington smiled at Kit, then gestured for Elaine to take the seat next to her. Kit took that to mean they were going to have a little heart-to-heart, so she turned her attention to her tea guests.

Elaine sat obediently in the seat next to the headmistress, who said to her, "I've been asking a lot of you lately—tutoring Katherine as well as all of your other responsibilities. But the reason I've asked so much of you is that you are a model Covington student."

Elaine almost fainted with relief. The color rushed back into her face, and she beamed her most modest smile. "Thank you."

"Even now, as we pretend to enjoy this abomination of a tea, can't you see how much this girl needs your help?" Lady Covington tipped her head in the direction of the other guests. Kit was merrily moving from one to the next, interrupting every single one of them by piling more potato salad on their plates whether or not they asked for it.

Elaine tried not to show her revulsion. Kit's improper behavior was a disgrace to Rose Cottage. The headmistress did not deserve to be burdened with such a distasteful display. Fortunately, Elaine knew better. "I won't let you down," she promised.

Lady Covington nodded. "I know."

Elaine stood and picked up the pitcher of . . . Arnie Whoevers. She decided to make the rounds and show the headmistress how a proper English host served her guests at a proper English tea.

Josh was walking by the dining hall, minding his own business, when his nostrils were attacked by the most scrumptious smell. Not just beef in general, but that particular mixture of spices that meant someone in the dining hall had *hamburgers*. He hadn't had a hamburger since coming to Covington!

His nose led him straight to Rudy at the grills. There he spied a sight that almost made him cry: a plate of sliders. He could even see globs of creamy red ketchup oozing out from between the buns along with hints of sweet green relish. "Sir, I'm offering you the opportunity to totally make my day," he told Rudy, gazing at the sliders. "I smell home."

With a shrug, Rudy handed him the plate. "Here. I've already had six."

Josh took the plate. Yes! Ooooh, yes! And to make it even better, Anya was by the condiments table! He wandered over. "Is that your first burger?" he said by way of hello, indicating her plate. "Or is Friday burger night at the palace, you know, like—"

Anya shoved her burger into his mouth.

He thought she was just playing. He fumbled it out of his mouth and went on, "Is there, like, a dress code, like burger tuxedos or, like, royal ketchup or, you know —"

Anya glared at him. "Shhhhh! Secret, remember?" she whispered fiercely. "You promised! You swore on your life! I can't have people finding out *mmmbfff*—!"

Josh had stuffed the burger back into *her* mouth. "What?" he asked innocently. "We're just two kids eating burgers. I don't know what you're getting all wound up about."

Looking reassured that her secret was safe, Anya grinned and bit into the slider. Josh bit into his, savoring the taste of home, and they proceeded to eat and chat about other foods they missed.

The tea was over.

Kit felt drained, as if she'd just pulled off a major world event. *Hey, I did*, she thought. *This was a major event in* my *world! It so qualifies.* She straightened up as Lady Covington approached, ready to take her leave.

"Well," said the headmistress, "that was . . . interesting."

Kit tried not to smile too hard. "I'm glad you liked it."

"And I was impressed by how you handled Miss Whiltshire."

Uh-oh, Kit thought. "I, uh, don't know what you mean."

Lady Covington's eyebrows rose. "Working around her scheme must have been challenging. You handled it with surprising grace. Even while serving sss . . . slitheries . . . ?"

"It's sliders," Kit reminded her. For about the seventh time. "But if you knew about it, why didn't you punish us?" For some reason, Kit didn't feel awkward asking that direct question. The whole tea drama had closed some of the distance between them. They weren't buddies or anything, but Kit felt somehow closer to the headmistress. Something had been offered and accepted on both sides. That kind of sharing changed relationships. It was anybody's guess how the change would show itself in the days to come, but Kit had faith it would be good.

"Sometimes one must let these things work themselves out," Lady Covington said in answer to Kit's question.

"Totes," Kit agreed.

"Well, as much as I appreciate the experience of your version of our great English classic, I'm afraid I do prefer the traditional manner. How is next week? My office?"

Kit was busy comparing the two very different tea events in her mind. "Except this kind of tea is way more exciting," she concluded. Then she realized what she'd said aloud. "Oh! I didn't mean anything by that! Your teas are totally fun, too. I just didn't realize it was going to be a regular thing."

Lady Covington gave her a strange look, her eyes unusually warm, her smile softer. "Sometimes you remind me . . . of . . ." She almost laughed, then paused. "I'll see you at tea. Good day, Katherine."

Okay, that wasn't weird at all, Kit thought, watching Lady Covington head to the stairway that would take her back to her office. She was finding out just what her mother meant when she'd say, "People are onions, Kit. Layers upon layers upon layers."

Nav was pleased by how the day had gone. It hadn't been much fun sweeping classrooms and wiping windows for three hours, but with all the Juniper boys pitching in, Will's punishment chores for that day had been finished in record time.

And that wasn't the end of the story. Acting like a leader, Nav rounded the Juniper boys together again and led them to Lady Covington's office after tea. There was one last thing to do.

They stood before the headmistress's desk, hands folded, trying to look contrite. "Although noble, and a criminal mastermind, he did not act alone," Nav confessed on the group's behalf.

Lady Covington accepted the news by saying, "Your punishments are in your mailboxes."

Nav's jaw dropped. "They are?" The boys glanced nervously at one another. "But how did you . . . ?"

"All for one, was it not?" Lady Covington picked up her pen and began to write, no longer looking at them. "You're excused," she said.

Okay, that was just plain creepy. Nav and Josh exchanged big-eyed glances, and the boys all sort of shuffled backward toward the door, afraid of turning their backs on this woman who was somehow always aware of their every move. Was the school bugged? Did she hire spies? Nav doubted it. Her abilities could have only one logical source.

She was a *Covington*. Propriety—and its enforcement—were her superpowers.

"Dad?" Kit called. Where on earth was he? She had been searching for ten minutes now, checking his quarters by the stables, the tack room, the back courtyard . . . "Dad!" she called again.

TK stuck his head out of his stall and whinnied.

"Where'd he go, boy?" Kit asked.

TK shook his head and grunted.

"Hmf. You're no help." She headed for the main building, wondering if maybe he'd gone to see Lady Covington.

Rudy was in the dining hall. It was empty at this time of the evening, so he had set the lights low. Only one other person was in there with him: Sally Warrington. She sat before one of two place settings that he'd arranged at the far corner of the teachers' table. After finishing the last of the preparations, Rudy joined her there, placing two bowls next to the plates already there. The menu? Perfect grilled cheese sandwiches and two bowls of tomato soup. He had promised her a "nice meal." Well, this was his definition of a nice meal!

"Thank you for inviting me to tea," Sally said, examining the food with amused interest.

"I didn't invite you to tea," said Rudy, handing her a packet of oyster crackers. "I invited you to *supper*."

Sally laughed, though whether it was because of his comment or because of the crackers, he wasn't sure. "*Tea* is what we call this sort of casual evening meal," she explained. "Supper is quite formal."

"Tea in my world is that dark bitter liquid you people gulp down by the bucket."

Sally laughed again. Rudy decided he liked the sound of it. "How dare you, sir!" she said jokingly. "You could be sent to the Tower of London for saying such a thing!" In a low whisper, she asked, "And do you know what used to happen to the prisoners there?"

He pretended to think about it. "They made them drink lots of tea?"

That drew more laughter, and it was contagious. Rudy found himself chuckling as Sally said, "Nothing as delicious as all that."

Rudy relaxed with all the laughing and joking going on. It had been a long time since he'd laughed, really laughed. As for Sally, he figured she'd been born laughing. Her silly sense of humor suited her. He'd seen her behave in a formal manner with Lady Covington and various school benefactors, and he'd seen her strict side now and then when she'd dealt with unruly students, but she seemed most natural with a mischievous smile on her face and a giggle on her lips. His imagination conjured up an image of Sally with flowers in her hair, dancing with fairies in a classic English garden by moonlight—and then he mentally kicked himself for indulging in such a dumb idea. Holy cow, he really *was* acting like a teenager!

Kit was on her way to the headmistress's office when she heard laughter from the dining room. Curious, she peeked in.

There sat her father, having dinner with Sally Warrington! And from what she could tell, they were eating Kit's favorite meal, the meal her mother had always made on Friday nights for the three of them: grilled cheese sandwiches and tomato soup!

More laughter drifted from the couple. "How is it?" her dad asked Sally.

"It's delicious, Mr. Bridges."

"Do you think you could start calling me Rudy?"

Kit felt her heartbeat stutter. Was her dad . . . ? Did he . . . ? Was this the beginning of a . . . a *romance*?

She backed away. This couldn't be real. Her dad would never betray her mom! With her thoughts whirling, she ran out of the building and into the cool of the evening. She didn't even know where she was going. She just had to get out—"Oof!"

She'd run right into Nav. "Whoa!" he said. "Where's the fire?"

Kit felt her eyes tear up. Nav was looking at her with real concern now, but she just said, "I've—I've got to go!" and wiped at her eyes.

Nav reached out a hand. "What's going on?"

Kit ran.

Chapter 10

PARENTS AND OTHER COMPLICATIONS

The next morning at breakfast, Kit made it a point to sit at the table nearest the teachers' table. She wasn't hungry, so there wasn't really any reason for her to be there. Still, she kept glancing over to where her dad and Miss Warrington had been only hours earlier. In some strange way, it felt like they were still there. She hated the feeling but couldn't seem to shake it.

Anya joined her, setting down a plate filled with bright-yellow pineapple slices, plump red strawberries, a little pastry with a dollop of sparkling blueberry jam in the center, and a fluffy golden *pain au chocolat.*

Kit's plate held two pieces of toast. No butter.

"That is one sad breakfast," Anya noted.

Kit shrugged with one shoulder. "It doesn't want to talk about it. It's in a mood."

"Weren't you supposed to be eating pancakes with your dad this morning?"

The operative words being "supposed to," Kit thought sourly. Before she could say anything out loud, though, Josh sat down with them. "Miss Warrington was seen walking across the grounds last night after dark *with a man,*" he reported.

Oh, terrific, Kit thought. *It's already gossip.*

"No!" said Anya. "Was it Mr. Griffin? I saw Mr. Griffin whistling yesterday. Grouchy Griffin *whistling!*"

Kit wanted to hide under the table. "It wasn't him," she said.

As though she hadn't spoken, Josh continued to Anya, "Dude, yesterday? Mr. Peters was wearing so much cologne, my nose hairs curled up!"

Anya playfully swatted his arm. "Peters looks like a goat! Miss Warrington *wouldn't!* But"—she counted off on her fingers—"Minnie Minister told Jilly Jones, who also told Tara Wong that Mr. McCullough was buying flowers in the village."

"Please," Josh said. "He's, like, eight hundred years old. If he bought flowers, they'd be for his own grave."

"It was my dad!" Kit blurted out. "With Miss Warrington."

"Aww," said Anya. "So nothing scandalous, then."

"Bummer," Josh agreed.

"I wouldn't be so sure," said Kit. "They were eating grilled cheeses and making goo-goo eyes at each other." She tried to keep the anger out of her voice and failed.

Anya must have heard it, because she backed off. "Are you sure it was goo-goo eyes? Maybe they were making normal, respectful colleague eyes?"

"I know goo-goo when I see goo-goo," Kit said. "He was laughing, and he looked happy. He's probably even forgotten what today is."

"Is it International Sad Breakfast Day?" Josh quipped in an attempt to cheer them up again. "I mean, what *is* that on your plate?"

"That's exactly what I told her!" Anya laughed.

On any other day, Kit would have found the comment funny, too. But not today. "It's my mom's birthday."

It was like she'd dropped a Serious Bomb. Anya and Josh went from sunny to solemn in a split second. "Oh," said Anya. "Oh, Kit . . ."

Josh chimed in. "I'm sorry."

Kit accepted their apologies with a nod. "My mom had this tradition where she'd always do something that scared her on her birthday. So Dad and I said we'd do the same. Maybe going on a date was his classy way of honoring that." *Yeah, and maybe pigs have wings.* She suddenly felt sick. "I'll see you later." She had to get out of there—she needed air—she needed . . . something, something that didn't exist anymore like . . . *like maybe the family I used to have,* she thought.

She made it out of the building before Anya caught up with her. Dear Anya gave up her own breakfast and walked her arm in arm back to Rose Cottage, trying to cheer her up the whole way. "So you just tell me what we need to do to make today better, and we'll do it," she concluded when they reached their dorm room.

"I might try to trot TK over some poles for the first time," Kit said. "That should be completely terrifying. My mom would be thrilled. Want to come with?" She waited for Anya's response. She didn't get one—at least not the one she expected.

Anya stopped dead in the doorway. "Madhu!"

Kit peered into their room and saw a woman tidying Anya's bed. At the sound of Anya's voice, she turned, a pillow in her hands, and said with a bright smile, "Good morning, Your High—*Anya*!"

Kit felt renewed excitement. Maybe her own mother wasn't with her anymore, but here was the next best thing! "Is that your mom?" she asked Anya. It had to be! The woman was wearing a white-and-yellow sari, and she stood with such grace and authority that she could only be a mother. *No wonder Anya is so pretty*, Kit thought. *Her mom's beautiful!* She launched herself at the woman and gave her a big welcoming hug. "It's so nice to finally meet you!"

Mrs. Patel—as Kit immediately thought of her, since Anya was so proper that there's no way she should expect to call her by her first name—gave Kit a gracious smile, though there was a hint of something else in her eyes . . . confusion? Kit figured that was possible. She probably hadn't expected to get a hug from a complete stranger. But Mrs. Patel recovered and said, "Anya has told me all about you."

Kit grinned at Anya. "That's so nice!" Then to the woman she said, "But you, Mrs. Patel, are a bit of a mystery." Back to Anya: "Why didn't you tell me your mom was coming? I could have made my bed"—she used one foot to shove her pile of dirty laundry out of sight—"and picked up my clothes . . ." She expected Anya to laugh.

Instead, Anya seemed totally stressed out. "Uh, don't we have a meeting? And I'm sure Elaine has scheduled *something*. No? Anything?" She sounded frantic.

Why is she trying to get rid of me? Kit thought. Then it hit her—during the last year, Kit had been mourning the loss of her mother. She'd forgotten what it felt like to have to introduce your mom to your friends. It could be nerve-racking. *Anya's probably wigging out,* she realized, so she offered, "We have class."

"Class!" Anya cried. "Yes, that's right!"

The calm voice of Mrs. Patel brought everything back down to earth. "Would you mind giving me a few minutes with my . . . Anya?"

"Oh, of course," Kit said. She grabbed up her bag and asked her friend, "Meet you downstairs so we can walk to class?"

Anya nodded, and Kit left mother and daughter to talk.

With Kit gone, Anya faced the woman, who regarded her sternly. "This is how you greet me after all this time?" the woman asked. "Didn't I teach you better manners?"

Anya was so glad to see her governess, and now she could finally show it. "Madhu!" she cried, throwing herself into Madhu's waiting arms. "I missed you so much! But . . ." She stepped back. "What are you doing here? Is everything okay with Mother and Father?"

"They're both fine," Madhu replied, hefting up a garment bag and laying it carefully on a chair. "But there is an important ball they must withdraw from at the last moment. And so"—she unzipped the bag—"it is to be your public debut. This is what your mother selected."

Inside the bag lay a gorgeous *anarkali* dress of deep-red silk with sparkling gold-embroidered trim. Anya gasped at the sight of it. Then the obvious occurred to her: "But I can't. I have school."

"Lady Covington has excused you from afternoon classes."

"I can't!" Anya repeated. "My classmates don't even know who I am, I just—" She immediately stopped when Madhu held her hands palms up. She was a sweet woman, but she was also strict. As a governess, she had basically raised Anya from a little baby to the young woman she was now. Anya always obeyed her, not because it was expected or because it was the rule, but because she loved Madhu deeply. Madhu always treated her with firm but loving respect, and the two were almost as close as a mother and daughter. Anya would do anything for Madhu, but skipping class would damage the "normal girl" persona she'd so carefully cultivated since she'd arrived at Covington.

Palms still up, Madhu simply said, "It is your royal duty." Bowing slightly in a *namaste* gesture, she added, "Pardon me for saying so, Your Highness, but you may *not* say no."

Anya knew when she was beaten. And it wasn't that she didn't want to go to a ball or wear that spectacular dress. But keeping her rank a secret meant everything to her. What if someone saw her and guessed the truth?

She felt doomed.

Kit waited outside Rose Cottage until Anya joined her. Then they walked to class, chatting about Mrs. Patel and the fact that Anya had to skip afternoon classes for an important doctor's appointment she'd forgotten about.

"You're lucky you're escaping this aft," Kit said. "Did you see the new training schedule Elaine posted for the House Cup?"

"Is it brutal? She'll be in a fit for a while. The cup determines our first official league standings."

"You'd think we were going to the world championship. She wants us to go running at six every morning!"

"Hey, Kit!"

Kit turned to see her dad coming around the corner.

"Where were you?" Rudy asked. "I had a pile of pancakes as big as TK ready and waiting."

Thoughts of the House Cup and meeting Mrs. Patel and her upcoming history class blew right out of Kit's head, replaced by images of her dad and Sally eating dinner together and laughing. Her expression grew hard. "Thought you might be *busy*," she said sharply. "With something *else*. Or some*one*."

"Nope," said Rudy. "Just me and the barn cats."

"My mistake, then. Gotta go." Kit tried to walk past, but Rudy gently stopped her.

"Hey," he said softly. "It's me. Dad."

Yeah, it's you, Kit thought. *And it's me, and we don't need anybody else! It's like you're looking for ways to mess everything up!*

Rudy stared into her eyes. "Are you okay?"

"Just busy."

"How about after class?"

"Tutoring with Elaine."

Anya had a suggestion. "I got excused from classes today to spend some time with Madh— my mother. Perhaps you could request the same for Kit?"

No! Kit thought. *Anya, you don't know what you're doing!*

Rudy pointed his Stetson at Anya, pleased. "I knew I liked you, Anya." To Kit, he said, "Stand by, kid. I'm making it happen." He headed for Lady Covington's office.

Kit hated feeling angry at her friend, but she

just couldn't hide it. "Gee, Anya. *Thanks*," she said sarcastically. There was nothing else to do now but go to class, so she did, turning her back on her roommate, who clearly had no idea of the trouble she'd just caused.

"You're welcome," Anya called after Kit, delighted that she had helped. She had hardly gotten the words out when Josh appeared and pulled her aside.

"Spill, dude," he said eagerly. "Is there some kind of a maharaja-queen-lady here today or something?"

"Just my governess," Anya replied. "Kit assumed she was my mother, and I just kind of rolled with it."

"Whoa, what's she here for?"

Anya trusted Josh, so she confessed, "It's dreadful! They're making me go to this horrible royal charity thing tonight. I'm dying of nerves!" She wasn't pleased when Josh laughed.

"Whaaat?" he said, snorting. "Do you have any idea how many people would, like, die to be in your shoes right now?"

"I won't know anyone there!" Anya complained. "Who will I talk to? And who will make sure I don't get lost on my way to the loo? These palaces are extraordinarily confusing—you can't understand. And first I have to get out of here without anyone catching on!"

"Maybe you need some backup."

Anya was preoccupied debating her options. "Do I have time to dig a tunnel? Or should I fake an injury and call in the paramedics?"

Josh just shook his head. "You're really not good at this double-life thing, are you? Okay, look. What you need, Princess Dude, is a wingman."

Anya was at the end of her tether. "I don't have one of those!"

"Um, yeah, yeah, you do." Josh pointed to himself. "You know? Distract? Misdirect? Smoke screen?"

Anya wasn't getting it.

"Look, I've got it all covered. C'mon." Josh threw his arm around her shoulder and got them both to history class before the bell rang.

Rudy entered Lady Covington's office and took the seat in front of her desk.

As for Lady Covington, she appeared extremely

busy, moving from table to table to gather up folders and papers until she had a handful. Rudy knew from experience that asking for a favor when the head-mistress was busy might earn him a lecture, but he felt this situation was worth the risk. Kit was worth the risk.

"What could possibly be so urgent that it must interrupt my schedule?" Lady Covington inquired, sitting down and shifting the folders and papers around as if to emphasize how busy said schedule was.

She seemed a little more than busy to Rudy. Her voice was unusually sharp and crisp, her motions abrupt. She probably had an important meeting or something, and he was only adding to the pressure. Well, that was just too bad. Rudy felt that his request was as important, perhaps more important, than mere school matters. "Could Kit have afternoon classes free today?" he asked. "Please?"

"Is she ill?" the headmistress responded. "She ought to see the nurse."

"Oh, no, no, no, it's nothing like that. It's just . . ." Rudy cleared his throat, annoyed at himself for feeling so nervous. "Today is her mom's birthday."

Thinking it over for only a few seconds, Lady

Covington stated, "That is not a sufficient excuse for absenteeism. Good afternoon." She turned her attention back to her papers and folders.

Rudy sat there, stunned. When he'd been a kid, he'd never liked being shut down by an adult, especially when they assumed that what was important to him wasn't important at all. He felt that way now, and he didn't like it one bit. "Excuse me," he said, rising to his feet so that he was the one to look down at her. If she wanted to play I'm Bigger Than You Are, he could do the same. "This kid lost her mother. I'd like to spend some time with her, share some memories—"

Lady Covington gazed up at him with tired eyes. "That is what weekends are for."

Rudy decided to set down his Stetson before he accidentally ruined its shape by squeezing it in a sudden fist. "Let me get this straight—I'm supposed to tell her not to feel anything until it's *convenient*?"

"You may wish to choose some different words, but that is the essence."

"She's a *kid*. Without a *mom*. She misses her. And frankly, ma'am, so do I." Rudy's voice quavered with emotion on that last bit, but instead of feeling embarrassed about it, he felt proud. He had loved his wife, Elizabeth, more than Lady Covington would ever know. He would never ever be embarrassed by *that*.

Lady Covington seemed to be in her own world, one that did not apparently include affection for others. "Many people miss many people, Mr. Bridges," she stated. "It does not excuse them from their duty. We are here to show these *kids* how to excel. Up to this point, your daughter seems to excel only in causing chaos and exhibiting zero respect for authority."

"Okay, so Kit can be a handful," Rudy had to agree. "She's spirited, like her mother, but—"

"You are also a faculty member," Lady Covington went on. "I do not excuse faculty members without notice. Certainly not to 'share memories.' Is that how you think things operate around here?" In a scolding tone, she added, "*Really*, Mr. Bridges."

That was it. Rudy had to exercise extreme control to keep his temper in check. But he let the anger burn in his eyes as he said, "Thank for your time." He picked up his Stetson, adding a reluctant "Ma'am" before heading for the door.

"Mr. Bridges."

Rudy paused but didn't turn around.

"I am sorry for your loss." Lady Covington's voice carried a softer tone, but Rudy still felt it wise not to respond. He didn't trust his own voice to come out soft at all. So he nodded and left.

Chapter 11

A BITTERSWEET BIRTHDAY

Sally Warrington's English students sat around waiting for their teacher to arrive. Kit's desk was behind Nav's, so they automatically began a conversation. "I saw your horse in the pasture this morning," Nav said. "He was fleeing from a duck. He's quite the challenge to tame."

Kit screwed up her face. She hated to hear about TK's weirdness, especially now that she was to compete in the House Cup. But she tried to convince herself that knowing these things was at least better than *not* knowing them. Still—TK ran away from a *duck*? "I can barely tame his mane," she said. "He looks like he's had an electric shock half the time."

"Wet his mane," Nav suggested. "Put in some tiny braids once or twice a week. It'll get retrained."

"Ooh, thanks! I wish all his other issues were that easy to fix."

Nav turned more in his chair so that he could better face Kit. "Try me."

"I think he's scared of red. The color. Every time I try to walk him even near the red-striped poles in the ring, he freaks." Kit paused and glanced to her right. Will, sitting several rows away, was looking at her. He quickly looked away, and she resumed talking to Nav. "Plus he tried to eat Anya's red sweater, and once he pooped in a red flower bed and—"

Nav stopped her there. "That is quite a solid collection of evidence."

"I have to convince him not to hate on red, or he'll never jump!" Kit went on. *And I'd better hope there are no ducks in the ring during the cup, either, or I'll have a double freak-out on my hands,* she thought.

Kit's worries slid sideways, however, when Nav said, "I'm sorry to inform you, but horses are not able to see red."

"What? C'mon!" If it wasn't the color red, then what was TK's problem? Sweaters, flower beds, and ducks?

Sally entered the classroom, her arms full of reference books. Kit caught the title of one of them:

Eighteenth- and Nineteenth-Century Literature: A Critical Analysis. She steeled herself for a dull class hour.

It wasn't that she disliked literature; it was just that she found it hard to relate to the Brontës. They were a famous trio of nineteenth-century sisters who wrote the kind of romances that the BBC always turned into long, lavish TV series. Kit read some of the notes Sally had already written on the blackboard: *Why did the Brontë sisters use pseudonyms when they published their work? Which Brontë sister wrote* Jane Eyre*? Which Brontë sister wrote* Wuthering Heights*?*

All Kit wanted to know was how women in those days could breathe while wearing fourteen layers of petticoats. She was so happy she lived in a time that *didn't* involve corsets.

"All right," said Sally, "in your seats, everyone! We have a lot to cover today!" She set down her books. "Katherine Bridges? May I speak to you for a moment?"

Surprised, Kit went up to the front desk.

"I understand it's a very important day for you," Sally said quietly.

"I don't . . ." Kit got nervous. "I can't . . ."

"You need to mark this day," Sally told her. "It's important. Someone is waiting for you in the tack room. Someone who shares your feelings."

Kit grinned but couldn't move.

"Go on, then," urged Sally. "Quickly!"

Kit gathered her stuff and hurried out as Sally said to the class, "Right! Open your textbooks to page twenty-nine . . ."

Kit hesitated just outside of the tack room. So many emotions were roiling around in her chest that it actually hurt. Now that she had a moment to devote her undivided attention to her mother's memory on this most special of days, she just felt sick with grief.

Maybe that wasn't entirely true. Sally had been so kind to her just now that Kit also felt happy to have such a sweet adult friend—even if that friend did make her read classic literature. And even though Kit had left her pal Charlie behind in Montana, she had made so many new wonderful friends at Covington. Plus, her dad was waiting right through the door for her.

She couldn't really wrap her head around the fact that her dad had also become a *friend* during the past year. She had always loved him like crazy, but as a *dad*. Somehow he had managed to create a new dual identity with her, Dad plus Pal. The two didn't always overlap. Dad was still the authority, though he could also be fun. Dad-Pal was a new person, a guy who saw her as a young lady, not just a daughter for whom he was responsible. Dad-Pal treated her as an adult, let her take chances, cheered her when she did well, and helped her back into the saddle, sometimes literally, when she failed.

Oh, it was all so weird! She shoved the ugly roiling emotions down and let the anticipation of seeing her father fill her up with joy. That's what her mother would have wanted, and that's what Kit wanted, too.

She stepped into the tack room.

"There's my best girl," Rudy said, pushing his Stetson farther back on his head. Kit saw his cute crooked smile and smiled back—sometimes he could look just like a little kid!

"Hi," she said a bit shyly. She felt bad about skipping out on pancakes and for brushing him off when he asked about it.

But Rudy seemed to have moved on. "Well, kid," he said, removing the Stetson and setting it down, "are you ready to toast the most wonderful person we've ever known?" He picked up two glasses hidden behind him and handed one to her.

"Are those"—Kit studied the dark glop inside—"Mom's mud pies? In a *glass?*"

"She always did something that scared her on her birthday."

Now Kit got it. "And nothing's scarier than your cooking, Dad."

Rudy laughed, a laugh definitely aimed at himself. They sat down. "Oh, before you start . . ." He picked up his Stetson again to reveal something hidden underneath.

Kit recognized the object immediately. "The Ugly Brooch!"

It was indeed ugly. About the size of Kit's palm, the brooch was an orange-tinted glass flower with some kind of sparkly blue-green leaves on one side and a sweeping silver . . . thing . . . on the other. A little horn stuck out from the bottom. At least, it looked like a horn. Kit's mom had never been able to identify exactly what it was supposed to be. All together, the thing was garish and ugly. Truly, honestly, mind-bogglingly ugly.

Kit's mother had loved it for exactly that reason, and she'd hauled it out and worn it on her birthday every single year. *Funny,* Kit thought. *She never told us where it came from.* Kit presumed it was something her mom had found in a thrift store. *I hope she didn't pay more than a dime for it.*

Rudy was still holding the brooch out to her. Kit shook her head. "I am not wearing that horror show!"

"Somebody has to. It's a tradition. It looks lousy on me. I already tried."

Knowing that it was hopeless to resist, Kit took the brooch and pinned it on. It looked even uglier against the deep blue of her Covington uniform blazer. *Mom would be so proud!* she thought.

"I wasn't sure you'd show up," Rudy confessed. "You had kind of an attitude this morning. Everything all right, kid?"

Kit couldn't look him in the eyes. Now that Sally had been so kind to let her leave lit class, Kit was no longer in the snit she'd been in earlier about her dad's dinner date. Maybe she was jumping to conclusions. Even if she wasn't, maybe she was being unfair by expecting her dad to stay exactly the way he was. He had the right to reach for happiness, too. She was the one who always said change was good, wasn't she? Who was she to judge?

So she explained her recent behavior by saying, "Just . . . teenage mood swings. You probably don't remember them because it's been sooo long since you've had one. You know, with you being ancient and all."

Rudy gave her one of his special wide grins and chuckled. Then he grew serious again. "Missing her doesn't get any easier, does it?"

Kit met his sad eyes and shook her head. It didn't.

But they were there together, so they clinked glasses and sampled Rudy's horrible cooking.

"It's not bad," Rudy decided.

Kit tasted the smooth portions of chocolate and crunched down on the pie crust pieces. She didn't drop dead from it, so she said, "Could have been way worse."

After they finished eating, Kit asked her dad to walk her back to the main building to pick up her homework assignment. They ambled across the grounds under a gray English sky, but Kit felt warm sunlight in her heart. She could tell that her dad felt the same way. By the time they entered the main building, they were giggling at each other.

"I did *not* love the birthday when she insisted on the terrifying hot-air balloon ride," Kit recalled fondly.

"I'll never forget the shade of green you both turned before you barfed into the picnic basket!" Rudy laughed.

"It would have been less sad if we'd even made it off the ground!"

"You both did it, though," Rudy reminded her, "just like everything else you put your mind to. You're just like her in that way." He put his hand on her shoulder and smiled down at her.

My dad, Kit thought happily, gazing back up at him. *My dad-pal. My dad-dad-pal-favoritest-person-in-the-whole-world —*

Rudy looked up at the sound of approaching high heels. "Lady Covington," he said.

Uh-oh.

"I was stopping by to suggest that, instead of homework hour, Katherine might join you for a time." The headmistress frowned. "But I see you have disobeyed my rules in any case."

"She'll make up her classes," Rudy promised.

Lady Covington stared at Kit's uniform blazer. "What is *that*?"

"Oh," Kit said when she understood what the headmistress was staring at—the Ugly Brooch. "Horrible, isn't it? It was my mom's. She always wore it on her birthd—"

"Please remove it," said Lady Covington. She sounded almost angry.

Rudy clearly had had enough of the headmistress's haughty attitude. "Oh, come on," he began, getting revved up.

Kit felt a possible argument about to explode, so she said in her most reasonable tone, "Dad. It's fine. It *is* against regulations." As she took it off, she couldn't help but whisper to him, "But it was worth it!"

Lady Covington was not amused. "In the future," she said, "you may both do well to remember that TK is here because I permit him to be. And I may revoke that permission whenever I choose."

"Lady Covington . . . !" Kit began, but didn't know what else to say. She and her dad were already very much aware of the TK situation. Why did the headmistress need to ruin her mom's birthday by bringing it up?

"You would also do well to remember that *you* are both here because I permit you to be." With that, Lady Covington left, the *click-clack* of her heels fading away around the corner.

Kit wanted to cry. What was wrong with that woman? What was the point of being so mean? How in the world could anybody ever become so . . . so *awful*?

Chapter 12

PAPARAZZI, LOGS, AND OTHER HURDLES

Anya had spent almost two hours getting ready for the charity ball. She took a bath, then Madhu painted her nails, did her makeup, and styled her hair. Anya donned the gorgeous red *anarkali*, slipped on matching heels, clasped an intricate diamond necklace around her neck, put on diamond stud earrings, and then, finally, Madhu affixed a beautiful gem-studded *maang tikka* to her forehead.

When Anya entered the main building, a coat draped across her shoulders to hide her outfit, nobody was in sight. That was the idea. At this time of the evening, everyone would be at dinner, so the corridor was safely empty.

Well, there was one person there, waiting for her: Madhu. "Oh, you look beautiful, Princess Anya!"

the governess cried upon seeing her. "Are you ready to go?"

"Thank you, Madhu," said Anya, "but there's just one thing . . ."

On cue, Josh stepped out of hiding dressed in a tux. "I scrub up pretty good, eh?" he asked, preening.

Anya drew in a quick breath. He certainly did scrub up good. Josh Luders scrubbed up *really* good!

"Anya." Madhu's voice took on a judgmental quality that Anya knew all too well. It meant that something traditional was not being done traditionally. "Who is this?" the governess asked, eying the young man before her.

"Madhu, this is Josh."

Josh smiled and waved.

"He will be my escort for this evening." Anya hoped that by making the news a declaration of fact instead of asking for permission, she might get her way.

Alas, Madhu's job was to see that the royal princess followed the royal rules. "This is highly irregular," she pointed out. "Your parents would expect to approve anyone who would accompany you."

"I accept that it's my duty to honor my parents' expectations, but that doesn't mean it's easy," Anya said respectfully. "It will genuinely help having Josh with me for support."

What happened next totally surprised her. Josh politely took Madhu's hand and kissed it. "I'd do anything I could to help your charge, ma'am," he said. Anya had never heard his voice sound quite so . . . adult! As much as she liked goofy Josh, she rather liked this side of him as well.

Madhu mulled it over. "Loyalty is a quality the family values deeply," she said. Then she smiled the smile of a woman who knows when she's being buttered up. "You may join her." With a formal nod, she turned and started down the hallway.

Behind her, Anya and Josh exchanged triumphant fist bumps.

"I saw that!" Madhu said, her back still to them. "You will exhibit behavior worthy of the *maharaj kumari* from this point forward, young sir."

Anya and Josh exchanged silent giggles as they followed, trying their best to look like a proper royal couple.

Meanwhile at dinner, Kit set her plate down at a table, then went to get a drink. When she got back,

Nav, who was sitting nearby, said, "I had a thought about TK's phobia."

"Awesome," said Kit. Then she noticed a yellow sticky note by her plate. It hadn't been there before. It read, *I have a surprise for you and TK. After dinner. Stables.* It was written in the same neat block-style lettering of the previous note.

Kit looked up at Nav, but he was busy pushing peas around his plate. Kit wondered if he was just having fun, leaving notes and telling her little hints while playing innocent about it. She decided to play along, say nothing for now, and then meet him at the stables later.

Boys are so weird, she thought.

Josh was in heaven. He was riding in a limousine with a lovely young girl who was his friend—not his *girlfriend*, just girl-who-was-a-friend—and they were heading for a party that was sure to be the fanciest event Josh had ever attended. Oh, and they were going to be the center of attention, too! Things couldn't get cooler than that!

So why Anya was so tense?

"Okay," she was saying, wringing her hands, "best-case scenario? Nobody notices me, and we get to eat a thousand desserts. Worst-case scenario? Everybody notices me when I trip over my *pallu*, fall into the buffet, and spill gravy all over Prince Harry . . . *and* it gets covered by the evening news, and everybody at school sees it!"

"You forgot the sprinklers going off and my pants splitting," Josh added helpfully. "Catastrophize much?" He liked the word *catastrophize*. He'd learned it as a kid by looking up the word *catastrophe*—one of his favorites—and checking to see how many different forms it could take. *Catastrophize* had won him quite a number of arguments because few people had even heard of the word. The takeaway lesson? *What* you said in an argument was important. *How* you said it was even more so!

Anya wasn't in the mood to appreciate a new word. "And then I'd be a social outcast!" she exclaimed.

Josh couldn't stand to see her so riled up, especially when there was no reason for it. "Look, you don't have to worry, okay? You've totally got this." He placed his hand over her hands to stop them from fidgeting. "You were born ready, like, literally, because you were born a princess." How cool was it to know a real live princess? And such a nice one!

Anya tried to compose herself. "You're right. I am Princess Anya Patel, and I can do this!"

The limo stopped. They had arrived at the party venue. The second the driver opened Anya's door, Josh heard people clapping and cheering for her. She got out, and Josh scrambled quickly to join her. How many times would he ever get this kind of attention, from paparazzi, no less?

Flash! Flash-flash! "Smile!" said the reporters. *Flash-flash-flash!*

Josh squinted at the bright camera lights, then realized that, no, he should relax his facial muscles and look poised and confident. The last thing he wanted was to look like a dork in the photos. They might end up online or even in the newspapers! He pretended that he was a prince and stood as regally as he could manage, slipping his arm around Anya's shoulders and giving his adoring admirers his finest royal smile.

After dinner, Kit pulled on a warm knit sweater and went to the stables. No one was around yet, so she visited TK. "Hi, boy." She stroked his soft, warm nose. "How are you doing? How was your day? You know, eat hay, drink water, poop, eat again?"

TK nickered.

"Yeah, that must have been great."

Nav popped his head out from around the corner. "Kit! Excellent timing!" He held up a book. "This is *The Hilary Whistlepot Guide to Technical Riding*. It's full of tips for taming a horse with . . . uh . . ."

"Issues?" Kit suggested.

"Quirks," Nav said. "We'll call them quirks." He handed her the book.

"This is perfect! Thanks!" Kit held the book up to TK. "See this, TK? I'm going to read you every page." She had to pull it away, though, because TK wanted to eat it. When she turned back around, she noticed Will standing several stalls away.

"Hi," Will said. "Sorry. Didn't meant to interrupt."

Kit's mood dropped when he spoke to her. She could barely forgive him for just walking away from her when she'd tried to explain why she was so upset—let alone forgive him for playing a role in Rudy getting hurt and sending her back to square one with TK. "It's fine." She expected Will to walk past them to finish going to . . . wherever it was he was heading, but instead, he gestured to the door.

"There's something, uh, something in the paddock I think you should see."

How was it that every time she talked to Nav in the stables, Will showed up? What was he trying to prove? "I'm busy right now," Kit said.

Will wouldn't let it go. "Uh, your dad says you should come. And if you could tack up TK . . ."

Kit felt like she was being manipulated, but if her dad said to come, maybe it was important. She let Nav help her tack up TK while Will stood back and waited. Then all three of them led the gelding outside.

Kit saw her dad waiting under the big floodlights that illuminated the practice ring. His injury was much better now. He still wore the walking boot and would continue to do so for a few more weeks, but he rarely used the hated cane anymore. He was using it now, though, probably because it was nighttime. One little slip or trip could undo all the healing, so Kit was grateful that he was being careful.

He gestured at what looked to be a homemade jump course. Instead of poles, jumps were made with piles of logs and tree branches, many still covered with deep-green moss.

"They're not striped," Will explained, "so they look like things TK knows, things he's seen in the pasture."

"This way, he gets used to trotting over poles," Rudy added. "Generally. It's desensitization."

Now Kit understood. "This is awesome. Thanks, Dad!"

"All I did was watch Will heave a few branches around."

Nav was studying a sturdy jump made out of three long logs held up by two bales of hay. "It's an inspired idea, Will."

"Yeah," Will said, and turned to Kit. "And then you work up to the striped ones, and he won't even notice. Hopefully."

Kit liked the practice jumps, but she wasn't ready to look at Will yet. She just couldn't do it. From the corner of her eye, she saw him step back in disappointment.

"Oh, before you go back out there," said Rudy, digging in his pocket for something, "put this on. For good luck." He handed Kit the Ugly Brooch.

Nav saw it and said with heavy sarcasm, "Oh, my. That is quite something."

Kit laughed as she pinned it to her sweater. "It was my mom's."

"Oh." Nav shrugged. "Well, you know what they say—you can't choose your family heirlooms."

"They say that, huh?"

Nav nodded, trying to keep a straight face.

Kit would have enjoyed taking the joke further, but her dad chose that moment to lean in and whisper, "Will worked real hard on this."

Great. Now Kit felt guilty. Was she supposed to feel grateful? She had still been focused on her lingering anger, but this was a really nice thing he'd done for her. Which emotion would be the victor? Forgiveness was the most important, Kit knew that, but it wasn't as if Will had even apologized. Then again, perhaps this jump course was Will's way of doing so. Words weren't the only way to apologize. *And let's face it,* she thought. *Will is not big on words.*

"Will?" she said, and she made herself look directly at him. "Thank you. It doesn't make everything okay but—"

Will interrupted her, putting her out of her misery. "Should we see if TK likes it?" he suggested.

Kit nodded. "I think we have to."

Will had been holding TK's reins, keeping the horse calm while everyone talked. Now he handed the reins to Kit. She mounted TK and rode him to the starting point while Will and Nav moved to the rails to watch.

"You got this, kid," Rudy said as Kit began with a comfortable walk. "Beautiful. Keep his rhythm even."

"Okay, heels down, hands light," Kit recited to herself. She sat straight in the saddle but not rigid. She loosened her death grip on the reins and tried to settle her emotions so that TK would feel confident under her command.

"Keep breathing," Rudy advised her. "And don't worry."

TK was approaching the first obstacle: a small pile of branches. "We've got this, boy," Kit encouraged him. "There's nothing to be afraid of." She guided him over the branches. At the last moment, his back hoof clipped a branch, causing it to topple from the pile with a loud *clunk*!

TK kept going as if nothing had happened.

Kit wanted to shout out, "Yee-HAW!" but settled for a soft sigh of relief. Knocking over a branch was a small thing, but it could easily have spooked TK. Will had been right—TK knew what branches were and showed no interest in them whether they were stacked or not. *Excellent!* Kit thought.

Will watched Kit with pride. She always tried so hard, and Lady Covington gave her such a hard time. Lady Covington gave everybody a hard time, as far as he was concerned. But he was glad to be helping Kit, even if she was angry with him. It would all work itself out, he was sure of it, as long as he kept proving to Kit with actions that he really was sorry.

"What. Is. That?" came a familiar voice.

Will glanced over at Elaine, who must have seen the lights on in the practice ring and come to investigate. If something important was going on, she was always determined to be a part of it. "I would've thought you'd recognize a horse after all these years," he quipped. "Oh, he'll like the next one," he added, speaking of TK as he watched horse and rider.

Noticing how Elaine glared at Will and how Will ignored her, Nav explained, "Will created some special jumps to help TK."

They all watched as Kit guided TK around for a proper approach to the hay-bale jump. Up to this point, TK had calmly walked the course, but he suddenly picked up speed. Will and Nav gasped, and Rudy gritted his teeth as girl and horse actually *jumped* over the logs smoothly and cleanly.

"Whoa!" Rudy said when Kit wobbled a little in the saddle. "That's it, kid. Keep your balance!"

Kit was in her own wonderful little world. *We jumped!* she thought. *We JUMPED!* She was only vaguely aware of how far over she was leaning until she heard her father's warning. She straightened back up and walked TK over to her dad. "We jumped!" she said aloud, proud enough to burst.

Rudy laughed in delight. "Good! That's good!"

Kit thought it was more than good. *It's totally freaking amazing!* she thought. Before she realized what she was doing, she gave Will a huge smile.

He smiled back.

The front door of Covington's main building opened a crack, and Josh poked his head in. His eyes slowly swept from left to right.

All clear.

He opened the door wider to let Anya through, then closed the door behind them. They had agreed to return as quietly as possible, but as they tiptoed down the hallway, Anya let out a giggle. That made Josh snort. Before they knew it, they were laughing.

"Did you see how close I was to that Swedish princess?" Josh said, still feeling euphoric over the amazing evening he'd just experienced. "Like, I could have reached out and touched her nose!"

Anya gave him her best imperial stare. "You do realize that all those guards are not just there for decoration?"

"Yeah, but the point is, I *could* have, you know? I can't wait to tell the boys at home about this!"

"No!" Anya squealed. She faced him square on. "Josh, you promised. It's fine to be Princess Anya for a couple of hours, but just plain *me* goes to Covington . . . just plain *me* who isn't loved just because of her crown."

Josh felt his eyebrows arch high up on his forehead. "Y-you have a *crown?*"

Anya nodded.

"Okay, new deal. If you don't want me to tell anybody, you need to let me try that bad boy on." The minute the words were out of his mouth, Josh worried that he'd gone too far.

Fortunately, Anya knew he was joking. "I'm not quite sure it's your style."

"I don't know—any bling is kind of my style," Josh insisted, and then laughed. He liked teasing her. She understood his humor and returned zing for zing. He waited to hear what she would say as her expression went from wide-eyed amusement to sudden eye-bulging alarm.

"Elaine!" she whispered.

Before he saw her, Josh *felt* Elaine at his shoulder. He'd always had a natural built-in "authority detector" that warned him when a teacher or parent was nearby. It wasn't foolproof, but it usually worked well, and it had saved him from the consequences of many pranks. But he was rather disgusted to find that his "authority detector" reacted to *Elaine*. She was *not* a figure of authority, even if she was currently staring down her nose at Anya with an air of suspicion that would have made Scotland Yard proud.

"You missed another training session," Elaine accused.

If only it was anybody else, anybody but *Elaine*! Josh started to feel jittery and vulnerable, and that made him irritated. How did she do that to him?! Worse, he could see Princess Anya melting down into Student Anya, a much more timid version of herself, as Elaine's eyes drilled into her. Josh wanted to tell Elaine to back off and leave them alone. Then again, if this was about the House Cup, the girls needed to work it out themselves. He silently cheered Anya on as Elaine threw out another question that she had no business asking: "Where have you been?"

Anya floundered for a good answer, but it was clear she wouldn't think of anything fast enough to sound true. Josh blurted out, "Uh, the movies!" It wasn't his best lie, but if he stuck with it, it would fly. Hopefully.

Elaine didn't buy it. "Dressed like that?"

"What?" Josh challenged. "You know, sometimes a bro likes to look nice." He straightened his bow tie to prove the point. Elaine wasn't a guy, so let her argue *that* one!

Elaine surprised him. Like a wolf, she automatically zeroed back in on her weaker prey. "And you?" she demanded of Anya.

"An *anarkali* needs to be aired out every now and again," Anya said, "so why not tonight?"

Josh was so proud of her! Anya was definitely learning the finer arts of deception and evasion, something he figured every princess ought to know. Too bad Elaine thought of herself as deputy headmistress. "You know," she said, "I didn't care before, but now that I know you're lying? I'm curious."

Would this never end? Josh tried to give Anya an encouraging look, to let her know that she didn't have to continue Elaine's game, but even he knew there was no way out. He made a decision and flew with it. "Okay, busted!" he exclaimed. "It's just . . . look, Anya didn't want anybody to know, but I—I said, you know, no one's going to care, right? It's totally cool, right?"

Anya started to protest, trying to shut him up because she feared that he was about to divulge her secret. "Josh, please, no, no—!"

"Elaine, Anya is, uh . . ." Josh placed his arm around Anya's shoulder and pulled her close. "She's my lady." He rubbed Anya's arm, hoping that she'd get it and play along.

It took only a split second for Anya to catch on. "Yes, um, we were concerned that this would be a, uh, conflict of interest, with the competition coming up."

Elaine definitely seemed disappointed. "Oh, please. Do you think anyone's really interested in your sad romance?" She flicked her eyes at Josh. "With a *Canadian*?"

Josh's jaw dropped. Was there no limit to this vile she-monster's rudeness?

"I won't tell anyone," Elaine assured them. To Anya, she said, "Just don't share any of our team's strategies." She walked away with a flip of her hair, as if she'd just solved some great mystery and felt quite satisfied about it.

Josh was just glad she was gone.

"You genius!" Anya said to him, grinning from ear to ear. "I totally froze!"

"Ah, no extra charge," Josh said. "Plus, you're the best fake girlfriend I've ever had."

Anya bowed. "Thank you!" She paused. "Wait. How many other fake girlfriends have you had? Who are they? Do I know them?"

Chuckling, Josh linked his arm through hers, and they made their way down the hall.

Kit lay in bed, wondering how much time had passed. She had gone to bed at her regular time, eleven thirty, and Anya usually went to bed at the same time. They'd lay there in the dark and make stupid jokes about the past day's events until they fell asleep.

But Kit had gone to bed alone. She knew Anya had driven into London with her mom for some important doctor's appointment, but what doctor's appointment lasted all night? *Maybe they decided to make it an event*, she thought, snuggling deeper into her pillow. *They probably went to dinner, maybe did some shopping. Maybe they went to a movie. That's what I'd want to do if Mom took me into London. Dinner, shopping, and a movie, with lots of gabbing throughout!*

She sighed. Stupid, stupid, stupid. Now she was thinking about her mom, which only made her feel worse.

The dorm room door opened. Kit didn't move as Anya darted in, silently closed the door, and tiptoed to her nightstand. Kit waited until she figured Anya was just about to climb into bed, and then she bolted upright. "Hey, where the heck were you? I looked for you everywhere!"

Anya did a perfect impression of a deer caught in headlights.

Chapter 13

A ROYAL DILEMMA

I was with my mum!" Anya said, looking far too nervous. "I'm sooooo tired. Exhausted!"

Kit waited until Anya got into bed before announcing the big news of her day: "TK and I jumped today."

"Seriously? That's amazing!"

"It was an accident," Kit had to admit. "But I didn't fall off, and he didn't have one of his meltdowns."

"Oh, well done," said Anya. "That's total progress!"

"Yeah." Kit smiled, thinking it over. "So how was your day? What did you do?" She figured Anya wouldn't go into the icky details of the doctor's appointment. Blech. Who wanted to hear about that?

Thankfully, Anya must have thought the same. "Movies," she replied. "Dinner. Boring stuff." And with that, she settled down to sleep.

Kit remained sitting up. "Not so boring," she said wistfully. "Not when you get to do it with your mom."

"Yeah," agreed Anya.

Kit noticed the sad edge in Anya's voice and figured it meant she was showing sympathy for Kit's loss. *That's so Anya*, Kit thought. *She can't help but share how she really feels about things.*

The next morning at breakfast, Anya watched in wonder as Kit assembled her breakfast. It was like watching a kid play with building blocks. When she was done, Kit had a five-inch-tall breakfast tower on her plate.

"What?" Kit asked her roomie defensively. "It's just sausage, bacon, eggs, pancakes, whole wheat on the top and some kind of French toast thing on the bottom. And," she finished with a wave of her hand, "a sprinkling of granola."

Anya grimaced. "Interesting."

"Oh!" Kit said. "And chocolate spread, of course. Want a bite?" She slid her plate over.

Against her better judgment, Anya accepted the challenge. She gamely picked up the sandwich, struggling to keep the crammed contents from spilling out. "Is that chocolate spread really necessary?"

Kit acted shocked. "Are you really asking me that? Maybe we can't be friends. Try it!"

Anya awkwardly brought the enormous concoction to her mouth and was just about to take a huge bite when a voice barked, "Put! That! Down!"

Anya instantly obeyed, feeling a little bit relieved.

Elaine, dressed in a gray uniform shirt and sweatpants, stated, "That is not appropriate fuel for a run."

"Okay," Kit said, "I get that we're in training, but don't you think you're taking this cup thing a bit too seriously?"

"One jump doesn't let you off the hook," Elaine retorted.

"Of course not," said Kit. "And I promise you, I will eat, sleep, drink, and breathe the Covington House Cup. My rank will delight and amaze you."

"Good," Elaine responded. "Glad to hear it." She frowned at them. "Now run!"

Five minutes later, Kit, Anya, and all the girls of Rose Cottage, every one of them in a gray uniform shirt and sweatpants, followed Elaine down the hallway.

"I loathe running," Anya whispered to Kit as they all trailed Elaine like a bunch of ducklings.

To that Kit replied, "I loathe—"

Elaine glared back over her shoulder.

"—Elaine!" Kit blurted out.

Unaware of Kit's unintended insult, Elaine said, "At lunch, you're meeting me in the stables. I'm going to show you how to jump without looking like an orangutan."

"I don't think I'm going to be able to feel my legs by then," Kit said, and she wasn't kidding. Running track at school back in Montana had always made her legs go wobbly, and she had no reason to believe that moving those legs to England would make any difference.

Elaine, as usual, showed mountains of sympathy. "There's no getting out of it, Bridges."

Anya hated to see Kit get bossed around by Elaine. She knew Kit was in no position to argue about anything when it came to training for the cup. Lady

Covington had given Elaine full control over Kit's life in that respect. Anya had decided to say something to help Kit feel better when a hand reached out, grabbed her arm, and pulled her through a classroom doorway.

It was Josh.

Anya recovered from her shock. "Josh, I have to keep up with Elaine! Her eye's gone all twitchy, and I'm scared of what she's going to do to Kit—"

"Yeah, well, red alert," Josh interrupted. "Like, royal, regal red-carpet *alert*."

"I don't like the sound of that alert," Anya said as Josh handed her his mobile phone. She looked at the photo on the display. "That's us. From last night. Where did you get this?" It was definitely a photo taken by one of the paparazzi that had met them during their arrival in the limo.

Josh began to pace. "It was on Chirper. Some girl back in my old school saw it on some gossip website and forwarded it to me, and she was asking me who you are and where she can get a dress like yours."

"She liked my dress?" Anya asked.

Josh made a *grrr* noise of aggravation. "Focus! This is a serious secret-identity fail here! Like, how long before anybody sees this, right? And it could be anywhere! Everywhere! How long before someone *here* recognizes you?"

Anya panicked. "Delete it! Get rid of it!" she ordered, shoving the mobile back into his hands.

She couldn't bear what he said next: "You can't delete the Internet. All you can do is tell people the truth before they see it."

Anya gulped. "I can't! If they find out who I really am, my life is ruined! Everything will change! Trust me—I know from experience." She looked at him hopefully. If there was one thing Josh had proven to her, it was his ability to wriggle out of difficult situations. Surely he could come up with something to stop this train wreck!

But Josh shook his head. "Even I don't have a suggestion on how to get out of this one."

Anya refused to give up without a fight. "Josh, we have to figure something out. If Kit finds out that I've been lying to her all this time, she might never forgive me!" Kit was the most wonderful friend that Anya had ever made. To lose her because of a lie, a lie that Anya herself had maintained throughout that friendship?

She couldn't—*wouldn't*—let that happen.

The day of the House Cup was fast approaching. It was evening, classes were over, and Kit was looking forward to some downtime.

Elaine had other plans.

This is so not fair, Kit thought as she picked up a small plastic horse for the ninety-millionth time and slowly ran it along the perfect little model of a dressage ring. This was Elaine's latest exercise, playing with a model in an effort to help Kit remember her dressage test.

As an exercise, it was pretty clever. Dressage tests took place in a ring with letters around the edge. As Kit moved her toy horse around the ring, she had to tell Elaine what movements she would perform at certain letter points. This was supposed to help her remember the test when actually riding TK.

"At A, I do a working canter on the right lead," Kit recited. "Then trot at . . . E?"

"Incorrect," said Elaine. "You missed your twenty-meter circle. Again. From the start."

Kit felt as if they'd been doing this for hours. "Time out," she suggested. "TK needs a snack!" She galloped plastic TK along the table and made him leap headfirst into a bowl of popcorn. "Nom, nom, nom!" she said as TK "ate" the popcorn.

Elaine simmered silently.

Kit pulled the horse out of the popcorn, grateful at least that Elaine didn't tell her to stop horsing around. "They call it a dressage test," she said, "but it feels more like a math exam. How am I supposed to remember all this?" She reached for some popcorn.

Elaine slapped her hand. "Your score at the Covington House Cup *and* your score in the all-schools league *plus* my reputation *all* depend on you ranking high. Snack later." She stood up. "Doing physical work as you memorize will help it stick." She gestured at the floor. "Plank and recite your test."

"Who died and made you general?" Kit snarked, but she did as she was told. If she didn't, she would get a lecture from Lady Covington. *It's a sad day when a Bridges rebellion is so easily thwarted,* she thought, getting down on the floor. She assumed a plank position, holding herself parallel to the ground in a modified push-up position, and recited, "Enter at A. Working trot, track right at C, then . . . give me a sec." Her core muscles were screaming and were distracting her from the task at hand, despite Elaine's theory to the contrary. Her mind was blank.

"You need to ace this, or your donkey gets shipped away," Elaine said while examining the assortment of perfumes on Anya's dressing table.

"Does Lady C pay you to keep repeating that?" Kit grunted.

"I don't need payment to provide a stunning example to my classmates."

Kit had a good response to that, but she thought it wiser to keep things peaceful.

"Where is your roommate, anyway?" Elaine asked, still poking through things that didn't belong to her. "It wouldn't hurt her to join you."

That was it. Kit snapped, "Anya works just as hard as you do!"

"Is that before or after her secret rendezvous with Josh?"

That news made Kit give up on the plank position and drop to the floor. "Where did you get that idea?"

"I caught them sneaking out on a date."

"Did you torture them with six hours of planking to get them to confess? Because they are so not dating and you are so wrong."

"I'm afraid *you* are." Something about the way Elaine said that caught Kit off guard. There was no sarcasm or gossip lust in her voice. She had simply stated a fact.

Kit didn't know what to think.

Josh was trying to keep Anya from having a melt-down. "A few of my friends back home saw our pic online, but that's it," he assured her. He also thought that having this conversation in the middle of the hallway wasn't the smartest idea, but calming Anya was his first priority. He hoped nobody would hear them if they kept their voices low.

"My life depends on their ability to keep mum!" Anya freaked.

Josh struggled not to cringe at her volume. "Don't underestimate your boy, okay?" he said, indicating himself. "Like, I have stuff on everybody. They blab online, I blab online, you know? And I do know how to game the search engines to get their embarrassing results right to the top."

"Hey, what are you two whispering about?" Kit asked, joining them. She'd finally gotten away from Elaine and all that exhaustive planking and was in the mood for some gossip, specifically with the two people standing in front her. "I refuse to miss anything because Elaine likes to torture me with miniature horses."

"That's exactly what we were talking about!" Anya said.

Kit mentally went over the words she'd just spoken. "Really?"

"Really?" Josh echoed.

Anya gave Josh a look. Kit wasn't sure what kind of look it was, but Josh clearly did. "Yeah!" he suddenly agreed. "Yeah, miniature horses! Uh, fascinating fact, actually, the, uh, the ancient Romans had a breed of horse that was actually as small as, uh, as— as a house cat, yeah! You know, and they used to put it on people's heads!" He mimed placing a tiny horse on Anya's head while Anya smiled at Kit.

Kit raised her eyebrow. "Please, continue. I can't wait to see where this is going."

Now Josh was the one who was doubtful. "What, tiny horse hats?"

Okay, maybe Elaine was onto something, Kit thought. She'd heard some whopper fibs in her time, but tiny Roman horse hats? She had to get to the bottom of this, so she tried a different tack. "Hey, random question. Say we're going into town without a parent. Do we need a day pass to go into town? Say, to the *movies?*" Kit watched closely as Anya and Josh glanced at each other. *One . . . two . . . three,* she counted to herself, and then her two friends blurted out answers at the same time.

"As far as I know?" from Josh intermingled with "I'm not sure" from Anya.

"Huh," said Kit. "Okay. Elaine and I were just talking about it. About people going into town? To the movies? I thought you might know." She poured on the innocent charm the way she had smeared chocolate spread on her magnificent breakfast sandwich—the one she had never gotten a chance to eat.

Anya grabbed Josh's arm. "I have to get Ducky out into the field," she said at the same time that Josh pointlessly gabbled, "Uh, yeah, the thing, right, I know, yeah . . ." And then they both walked away as fast as they could.

Gotcha, Kit thought. Out loud, she said, "Good talk, guys! I'm so glad we can all be straight with one another!"

That just made them walk faster.

Kit sighed. When Elaine Whiltshire turned out to be more truthful than Anya and Josh combined, things were bleak indeed.

The next morning, Rudy asked Will to stay behind after breakfast. This had become something of a routine, so Will thought nothing of it. He took his time eating his own breakfast, then went up to the teachers' table after everyone but Rudy had left.

The equestrian supervisor had his list of things to do before the House Cup in front of him and a pen in his hand. "The stables need to be pristine," he told Will.

"Do we have a decade to do that?" Will asked sarcastically. The list of things to do was a page full of impossible jobs they had to accomplish in a very short time, and Will knew that Rudy knew it. They also knew they had no choice but to somehow make it happen, or Lady Covington would very likely barbecue them both on a giant spit.

"Nope," Rudy said. "Just a few days until the cup."

"When all the horses have to be show groomed?" Will noted. "What are we, a hair salon?"

"Apparently, we're the maids, too," Rudy griped. "The tack room's got to be organized. *Proper.*" He said the last word the way Lady Covington always said it.

It was a good thing that Lady Covington didn't appear to hear him as she swept into the dining hall. "Mr. Bridges, is everything all set for the Covington House Cup?"

Will held back a grin when Rudy replied, "Done and dusted, Lady Covington!"

Will couldn't resist chiming in, "And you should see the tack room, too. It's pristine."

"Excellent," said the headmistress. "This first league event will cement your reputation. It's very difficult to recover from a bad first impression. Nevertheless, I'm glad to see you have time to linger over your breakfast."

Rudy jumped to his feet. "Will and I were just going to go work out in the barns."

"Oh, really? I thought they were already spotless." Lady Covington turned to Will. "Will, see me in my office at ten, please?" She hurried away, off to her next executive duty.

Will felt as if lightning was now scheduled to strike him at precisely ten o'clock. "Do you think she's going to throw me a surprise party?"

Rudy gave him a sympathetic smile.

Later that day, as Josh was working at the tuckshop, his part-time job on campus, Anya took the opportunity to speak with him privately. "We need to be more careful, or she's going to catch on," she told him.

"To which thing?" Josh asked. "To the whole us fake-dating thing or the whole Princess Anya thi—"

"Don't say it! Either thing. Both things!"

As Anya said this, Kit dodged around a couple of students and slipped behind a wood molding that decorated the nearest doorway. That put her right next to the tuckshop, but neither Anya nor Josh could see her. She, on the other hand, could hear them!

"Well, then maybe we need to spend less time together," she heard Josh say.

"You don't want to hang out with me?" Anya asked. Kit detected hurt in her roomie's voice.

"No, I'm not saying that. Maybe it's just the right thing. For you."

"I just came to buy snacks! I wasn't asking to share your every moment."

Kit had heard enough. She popped out of hiding. "Ah-HA! You *are* dating! Why would you keep that from me? I thought we were friends." She glanced from Anya to Josh and back to Anya, wondering why the two of them seemed so distressed.

Anya stuttered nervously as she tried to explain. "I—I'm sorry. I'm so sorry. I'm really, unbelievably sorry."

"But why?" Kit asked.

"I—I just didn't want to make things awkward."

"Well, I'm not going to say you nailed that," Kit said. "Anyway, why would things be awkward? It's not like *I* want to go out with Josh!"

To which Josh exclaimed from behind the tuck-shop counter, "Hey! I'm right here!"

"It just hurts," Kit said. "Because other people knew first. I mean, *Elaine* knew." She was relieved when Anya seemed to understand.

"I promise," Anya said, "I will tell you anything you want to know."

Kit still felt left out, but she hoped that things would be better now. "Deal," she said. She was about to give Anya a hug when Josh leaped over the counter.

"All right, come on," he said. "Group hug. Come on, you know you want to."

Kit actually did want a group hug. If Anya was dating Josh now, that made Josh a closer friend to her. She gave her friends a hug. "Oh, Anya," Kit said afterward. "Could you meet me in the ring after class? I was hoping for some help."

"Anything for you," Anya said, though there was a strange note in her voice. Kit couldn't place it. It wasn't nervousness. There wasn't anything to be nervous about anymore. And it wasn't anger or sadness or anything that weird. It was sort of like . . . guilt?

Nah.

Chapter 14

THE HOUSE CUP AND HORSESHOE LUCK

Precisely at ten o'clock, Will stood before Lady Covington's desk. The headmistress placed his academic report card in front of him.

Will rarely thought about how many classes he was taking. It wasn't as if he had a choice about it anyway. But to see the long list stunned him for a moment: Drama, Mathematics, English Language, English Literature, Biology, Chemistry, History, Geography, Physics, and Equestrian. Was he really studying all those subjects at once? Add to that all the hours he spent working in the stables, and Will suddenly understood why he always felt tired.

"Are those grades acceptable to you?" Lady Covington asked him.

Will answered truthfully. "No, Lady Covington."

"You are dragging down the school's grade point average. This is unacceptable."

In his defense, Will said, "I spend a lot of time in the stable." She couldn't argue with that. It was true.

"That is not an excuse for this abysmal performance," Lady Covington responded harshly. "Ask your roommate. Ask Miss Whiltshire. Ask any number of other students who balance things successfully."

That wasn't a fair comparison. Nav didn't have a job, Elaine got tutored all summer so she practically knew everything before each school year started anyway, and everybody else—again, they didn't have to work in the stables. Will tried to make his point again. "I help a lot of students with their riding." Did she have any idea how many students rode as well as they did because *he* gave them advice and showed them useful tricks to manage their horses?

Lady Covington was not impressed. "Your ban from extracurricular riding will continue. I suggest you use the extra hours to study. Harder."

That was the last word, and Will knew it. "Yes, ma'am," he said.

"In addition, it has been decided that you will not ride in the Covington House Cup."

Will felt like he'd just been sucker punched. "But I need a rank for the Equestrian League—"

"Riding in the cup is a privilege. I will arrange for you to ride separately on a makeup day. That is all."

So that was it. Will knew he wasn't a very good student. After all, he'd already been kicked out of Tonbridge, Charterhouse, and Harrow. If he botched up Covington, where else could he go? His father would probably ship him off to Antarctica for the rest of his life rather than let him shame the family by attending a secondary school alongside England's unwealthy, nonelite children—his father had a rather unflattering name for them. How insulting.

There was no way to change things now, though. The best he could do was to tell the Juniper Cottage team his bad news and hope for the best.

He made his way to the practice ring where Rudy was working with Nav and Josh. As he neared the ring, he could hear Rudy say, "I think we got a shot at this."

Nav proudly stated, "We can defeat most of the other houses with our hands behind our backs."

Then Josh said, "But what about Rose Cottage? Elaine has been training them around the clock."

Will reached the ring as Rudy said, "Nah. We'll annihilate them! Are you kidding me? With the three of you, there's no way we can lose."

The moment had come. Will reluctantly announced, "I can't ride."

Rudy, Josh, and Nav all began talking at once. Will cut them off. "Lady C just banned me from riding in the cup." He leaned against the rails and wished he could just blow away in the wind. Just his luck—there was no wind blowing.

"She can't do that!" said Josh. "Dude, you're our best jumper!"

Rudy calmly said, "I don't understand. What happened?"

"My academics," Will said quietly.

"That's a little above my pay grade, son," Rudy said. "There's not much I can do."

Nav finally made the attack that Will was expecting. "How could you do this to us?"

"I didn't *do* anything to you," Will answered.

"Your failure affects the team! That's something that I consider when I set my priorities, which is why you've never seen me miss a single night of studying."

Will wanted to say, "Well, la-dee-dah for you," but not only would that be childish of him, he knew that Nav spoke the truth. Still . . . "Are you saying I deserve this?"

In answer, Nav maneuvered Prince toward the closest jump and urged his mount gracefully up and over.

Will just scowled at him.

Classes were over for the day. Rudy decided to clean up his desk in the tack room, but not because his desk was a mess. It was because Sally was there with Elaine doing an inventory of Rose Cottage supplies for the cup competition.

Elaine pawed through a box of tack. "Ten Rose Cottage blankets," she reported, setting them aside to see what was underneath.

Sally, standing next to her with a clipboard, checked it off on her list. "And how are we for Rose flags?" she asked.

As Elaine looked, Rudy took the opening to have a little fun. "Oh!" he cried in mock innocence. "Were those yours? I thought they were fancy bandanas! See, I've been using them to wipe my face—you know, I've been working *so* hard."

Sally gave him a smirk. "Very amusing, Mr. Bridges. You will not shake our team with your jokes. Right, Elaine?"

"Yes," responded Elaine, all business. "And we have ten flags, too."

Rudy was used to coaching students about horses, not adults about humor, but even he could see that Sally needed to work up some good old spirited team rivalry. "Come on, Miss Sally. This is the part where you say you've been using the Juniper Cottage flags as napkins for your bangers and mash festival!"

"Internecine rivalries ought to remain amicable," Sally stated primly.

Rudy wasn't even sure what that meant.

Sally explained: "There shouldn't be fighting between teams. We're all friends."

Rudy rolled his eyes. "Well, where's the fun in that?"

With a straight face, Elaine said, "I agree. That's why I used all the Juniper Cottage flags to line Thunder's stall."

"Ha!" said Rudy, pleased. "See? Elaine's got the spirit! I need an opponent here!"

Sally regarded him as if he were a year one student. "And you shall have one, Mr. Bridges—out on the field, where that sort of thing belongs." She turned on her heel and strode out the door with a smug "Ta-ta!"

Strange. As she left, Rudy noticed how she ran her fingers over a horseshoe that was nailed to the wall. No way could it have been an accidental move. She had touched that horseshoe deliberately. Why?

Rudy decided to find out.

As she had promised, Anya was ready to go meet Kit at the practice ring. If Kit wanted to try some jumps with TK, Anya wanted to be there to cheer her on. She had donned her riding gear and was just about to go outside when Josh rushed up behind her, grabbed her by the shoulders, and physically steered her around a corner.

Anya squealed in surprise, then snapped, "You are becoming a truly terrible fake boyfriend!"

"Has anyone said anything?" Josh asked her sharply. "About the incess-pray ing-thay?"

"Huh?"

"The princess thing—"

"Shhhhh!" Anya hissed. "No. Why?"

"Ducasse was on some random gossip website in the common room, and the picture was there. The Princess Anya one?"

Anya wasn't sure which part of her dropped lower, her jaw or her stomach.

"It's okay—don't worry," Josh said. "I completely contained it."

"You poisoned him and buried his body far, far out on the moors?" Anya asked, presuming that he knew she was just joking. Then again, it certainly would solve the problem. . . .

Josh replied, "Close. I bribed him with a whole box of chocs from the tuckshop. But I would go tell Kit, like, *now*, because this thing is only snowballing."

Anya shook her head. "I can't do that. I'll lose her forever. She's the first person who's liked me for who I am."

"Uh, hello?" Josh said, looking insulted.

Anya managed a smile. Josh had a way of making her smile even when she was upset. It was one reason on a growing list of reasons why she liked him so much. But him liking her? "Oh, come on, you didn't like me that much before you knew."

Josh shrugged, as if to say, "Well, of course! Why else would I?"

Anya gave him a playful swat and started to leave.

"Hey, where are you going?"

"I'm late to meet Kit!"

"Well, I got more chocolate bars if the bribes have to grow. Just let me know!"

While waiting for Anya to show up, Kit decided to give TK a pep talk. She walked him around the practice ring, leading him by his reins. "Okay, here's the plan. When Anya gets here . . . *if* she gets here . . . we're going to try out some jumping. Just at the baby height."

TK made one of his whuffling sounds.

"Yes, I know. You don't have to remind me of your quirks. But we can do this! It will be a team thing. If Anya would just help us—" She paused as she spotted someone approaching. "Oh, great. Wish for an Anya and wind up with an Elaine."

"What are you doing?" Elaine demanded. "Why are the jumps out?"

"Because I want to jump," Kit replied.

As expected, Elaine went snarky. "Yes, and I want to eat roast pheasant with the queen, but neither thing is happening."

"Yet," Kit said. She was about to add, "Hey, anything could happen," when Elaine quickly reached into her pocket. *Her phone must have vibrated*, Kit thought, and waited for Elaine to check it. If Kit knew anything, it was that she should never try to come between Elaine and her mobile. But Kit didn't expect to see Elaine look so surprised.

"I knew it!" Elaine said triumphantly. "Now the whole school knows, too!" She held up the phone so that Kit could see the picture—of Josh and Anya in formal dress, surrounded by photographers. "I told you they were dating," Elaine continued. "I'm always right."

Kit only glanced at the photo. What caught her eye was the caption. "Forget dating! This says *Anya* is a *princess*!"

Chapter 15

ELAINE THE INTERLOPER

Gripping TK's reins in a fist, Kit swept past Elaine and headed to the stables. She was angry. She was soooo angry! Anya was supposed to be her friend, and she never said she was a freaking princess? Only when TK balked, snorting nervously, did Kit realize that she'd started grumbling to herself, and it was frightening him.

She stopped walking, took a deep breath, and petted TK's forehead. "Sorry, boy," she said in a soothing voice. "I don't mean to upset you. And I'm sorry we aren't going to jump now. I just need to sort this out."

Calmly, Kit finished the trip back to TK's stall, removed his tack, gave him a carrot, and then headed directly for Rose Cottage. At first she thought her dorm room was empty, but then she spotted the tell-tale lump under her roommate's thick duvet. "I'm looking for Anya," she called out. "Actually, I'm not sure—that may not be her real name."

After a moment, a muffled voice said from under the duvet, "Of course it is!"

"Yeah, but you left out the *princess* part, which, *hello*, is kind of the most important part!"

Two hands appeared from under the duvet and yanked down the edge enough for Anya's face to show. "But it's not!" she said. "It's like *Miss* or *Mrs.* Or something. And I didn't do it on purpose."

Kit took in the fact that Anya was in bed. In the middle of the day. Fully clothed. "What are you doing in here?"

"The e-mail blanketed the whole campus, like a monsoon," Anya replied. She pulled the duvet back up to her nose, adding, "It was all I could think of to do."

"Fine. Whatever. I still can't believe you didn't tell me! Speaking of which, I totally forgot to mention I'm Dolly, a pop star posing as a student to gather material for my new album!" Kit struck a typical teen-star pose. "Crazy, right?"

Anya pushed the duvet off and sat up. "Listen, I'm sorry, okay? Can I at least explain why?"

"You can try. Sure." Kit folded her arms and waited.

Anya began softly. "I used to play with our cook's daughter when I was small, until I noticed that we only did what *I* said we should do. So the next time we played pretend, I asked *her* what *she* wanted to do—ballerinas or fairies . . ." She smiled at the memories, then grew somber again. "She told me that she'd always been told to let me choose."

That didn't sound like a problem to Kit. "I know, it's terrible when people are nice to you," she said.

"But that's not being nice!" Anya pointed out. "It's being . . . *not real*! It's fun to play what your friends want to play, too. And . . ." She sighed. "We kind of just stopped after that. Every time people find out that I'm a princess, on holiday or whatever, any kind of *real* friendship is over. They just want to borrow my jewelry or ask me about Prince Harry, and they stop telling me about themselves."

"I don't care that you're a princess!" Kit said. Didn't Anya get it? Social status like that was exciting, but it wasn't how Kit chose her friends. Her mom had always taught her that people are people and that everyone is equal. Sure, some have money and some don't. Some have lots of toys and some don't. Some are smarter than others, and some have better creative ideas than others. Everybody has different qualities, from physical appearance to beliefs to what they prefer to eat for breakfast. "But when the sun sets every day, we're all just people going to bed to dream our dreams," her mother would say.

"If you don't care, then don't be mad at me anymore. Can't you understand?" Anya asked her.

"That's the point!" said Kit. "I would have! Understood, I mean. But you didn't even give me the chance! I mean, *Josh* got to know! I know that he's your boyfriend and everything but—"

"About that." Anya squirmed. "He's not really, kind of, like my—"

"You and Josh aren't even dating?" Kit exploded. "That was a brand-new lie from, like, *today*!"

She fled the room. Maybe Anya was trying to be honest now, but why hadn't she started out that way? The very first thing they'd ever done together was go through Kit's belongings, item by item, when Kit unpacked after arriving at Covington. Kit had revealed her whole life to Anya, had answered every one of Anya's questions. And only now was she learning that "Anya Patel" wasn't the person that Anya had shown her in return. Was that trust? Was that honest friendship? No!

She could hear Anya running after her. "Kit, wait!"

Kit kept walking, forcing Anya to run to catch up.

"Kit, wait! When Madhu arrived that day—"

"Your mother," Kit said. "She's the queen! I didn't even curtsy!"

Now Anya looked positively guilty. "It's fine," she said. "That was my governess."

"What?" How many lies upon lies had Anya been telling?

They were standing in the dorm hallway, and the nearest door opened. It was Elaine's room, and she appeared, wearing a big smile. "Oh, there you are, Anya," she said, reaching out and taking Anya's hand. "I need to speak to you."

"Okay, yes, but I just need to . . ." Anya tried to pull her hand back, but Elaine didn't let go.

"It's really quite an ASAP situation," Elaine insisted, and pulled her into her room. "Come on!"

"But—"

The door closed.

Kit gave up and resumed her escape, muttering, "I need to think."

In Elaine's room, Anya was so overwhelmed by what was happening that she allowed Elaine to seat her in a chair. "Are you okay?" Elaine asked with concern, patting her shoulder. "I thought Kit was going to eat you alive."

Her mind still reeling, Anya looked at Elaine, almost seeing her but also still seeing Kit, a very upset and betrayed Kit. "You—you didn't see the picture?" she asked. Yes, the picture, the stupid paparazzi picture. That's what had messed everything up!

Elaine nodded. "Yes, it was quite flattering. Loved your hair." She reached out and stroked Anya's hair as if Anya were a big doll. "Do you want to go grab dinner?" As a joke, she added, "Before the boys eat all the good stuff?"

"Uh . . ." Anya wasn't even sure what room she was in. Where had Elaine come from, anyway? And where had Kit gone?

Elaine stood up, pulling Anya up with her. "After a tantrum like that, you need to give Kit a little time to cool off."

What tantrum was Elaine talking about? Kit's feelings were hurt, but she wasn't having a tantrum—

She got pulled out the door and all the way to the dining hall while Elaine chatted airily about this and that and the other. Anya didn't hear a word she said.

In the common room, Josh was studying his definitely-not-favorite subject, English, when Will swept in and sat down at his table. "All right," Will stated like a teacher, "your dressage is quite good."

Josh glanced up from his textbook.

"And your cross-country is quite brilliant, actually," Will went on.

Josh waited for it.

"But your stadium jumping is pretty shaky."

Ah, so that was it. "Kind of harsh," Josh commented. "But with the cup coming up, it's—"

"Exactly."

Josh had no idea where this was going.

"So?" Will prompted as if he'd been making perfect sense so far. "Meet me in the stables at four, and come prepared to work." That said, he hoisted his backpack and started to leave.

"Wait wait wait wait wait!" Josh knew that Will didn't offer his time and effort for free. There was something of value lurking in the shadows of this situation, and he wanted some. "What's in this for me?"

Will regarded him sternly. "A win?" he offered. "Plus, Nav needs to lose. So if I'm not in there, you're the next best thing."

So that was it. Nav had dissed Will earlier in the day about not being able to ride in the cup, so now Will was offering to help *him* so that *he* would beat Nav in Will's place. Clever. Josh just had to think of what he wanted out of this. A win would be good, but he wanted more than that. "Your room?" he suggested.

Will paused. "What?"

"It's the nicest one in Juniper Cottage. And my roommate is a total nightmare. So, you know, if I beat Nav, then you trade rooms with me."

Will acted like the mere idea was an insult. "Forget it."

"It's a small price to pay for me pounding Nav into the turf, dude!" Josh called after him, but Will just kept walking until he was gone.

Josh replayed the conversation in his head. It wasn't over. No, this meant too much to Will. He'd be back—Josh was sure of it. Reluctantly he went back to his English homework.

The next morning, Anya sat alone at a table in the dining hall, trying to enjoy her breakfast, but she had no appetite. She kept her eye on the doorway, hoping that Kit would show up. Not only was Kit missing this morning, but she hadn't even slept in their room the night before. Anya was scared that she had driven away the best friend she'd ever had.

A *pain au chocolat* appeared on a plate before her. Elaine sat down. "For some energy today," Elaine said. "You're going to need it."

"I thought you wanted us strictly on healthy foods."

"Unless one is in need of a little morale boost. Plus, I know that *pain au chocolat* is your fave."

Anya tried to smile, but she wondered why Elaine was being so nice. Elaine wasn't nice to anybody. But she had been there when Kit had stormed off. Maybe she was trying to make up for getting involved in their argument?

"So," Elaine said casually, "after the big photo reveal—wow!—is there anything I have to do differently around you? Like, use some kind of title?"

"Please don't," Anya said. "I'm still just me."

"Excellent! Well, speaking of morale boosts, the forecast for today is tip-top. And we've been working so hard that I thought we deserve a little fun. Let's go on a hack."

That sounded like a wonderful idea to Anya, if Elaine was being sincere. Taking a ride through the lovely Covington school grounds would soothe her nerves, and it would be good for Ducky. But one thing topped Anya's concerns for the day. "I thought I should speak to Kit. I think she slept in the barn." Anya hated the idea of Kit shivering under a horse blanket in TK's stall all night. If that was the case, it was her fault, and she wanted to fix it right away.

Elaine saw it differently. "She'll find you when she's ready. Come on. Let's go for a ride."

Anya had always thought that Elaine was mean, but her smile certainly seemed sweet and genuine. Maybe seeing the stupid paparazzi photo had actually opened up a door of potential friendship that might otherwise never have opened. Anya had to admit that she didn't really know how to deal with people very well. She had lived most of her life so protected. And that ride did sound nice.

She nodded her agreement.

Kit had indeed slept in the barn, much as Anya had imagined it. But unlike Anya, Kit had a lot of experience sleeping in rustic places. Her parents had run a horse ranch, after all. Little Kit had fallen asleep in sheds and barns and stalls, and she even remembered napping in a wheelbarrow once. Also, the family had gone camping quite often, so Kit had slept under the stars many times, on the ranch property and also in the nearby woods. Sleeping in a stall hadn't been a big deal to Kit except for all the hay she'd found knotted in her hair when she'd awoken.

"TK, did you do this?" she demanded while pulling it out strand by strand. It was as if somebody had deliberately woven each piece in!

TK tossed his head up and down, producing a low rumble that sounded suspiciously like laughter.

"Bad horsey," Kit scolded him.

After munching on a stale scone she found in her jacket pocket—a leftover from her last tea with Lady Covington—she didn't yet feel ready to return to Rose Cottage, so she decided to give TK a bath. She set up a bucket of water and a sponge and headed back to get TK, but she paused at the sight of a yellow sticky note on the door. This one read, *Take me with you! A real friend helps you do more than you dreamed of.*

She looked around to see who might have left it. The only other person in her section of the stable was Nav, who was about to muck out Prince's stall. "Morning, Nav!" she said.

Nav greeted her with a big smile. "Good morning, Katherine Bridges!" He gestured to her rolled-up sleeping bag and pillow. "Did you really spend the night out here in the stable?"

"Yeah, TK and I sort of had a sleepover. It's a long story." She fingered the note in her hand, wanting to just ask him outright if he had left the message along with all the others, but she suddenly felt shy. What a concept—a Bridges, *shy*!

Nav noticed. "Is everything okay?" he asked.

"Mostly," Kit replied. "Ish. Mostly-ish. But I did want to thank you for all your help." She tried to make her meaning clear by waving the yellow sticky around. *What is wrong with you?* she wondered of herself even as she did it, because it was clear that Nav had no idea what she meant.

"I try to be of assistance whenever I can," he said, watching her waving.

Realizing she looked like a jerk, Kit stuffed the note in her pocket. "TK and I *both* say thank you," she tried again. "I'm almost excited about the Covington House Cup!"

They smiled at each other, then both went back to work.

Neither of them saw Will appear from around Prince's stall. He frowned. Once again he had left a note of encouragement for Kit, and once again Nav had taken credit for it! He felt anger bubble up, but getting angry, he knew, was the wrong reaction. Confronting Nav would do him no good, either. The fact was, since Kit was going to compete in the cup, Nav had an advantage over Will—he had easier access to Kit, and he could impress her with his cup performance. Will had to find a way around that.

Luckily, he had one.

He put his shovel away and went directly to the dining hall. As he hoped, Josh was there, hungrily slicing into a pile of about eight blueberry pancakes smothered in syrup. Will headed straight for his table and said, "All right, the deal's on."

Josh stared at him, as though checking for any signs of deceit. "I get your room?"

"*If* and *when* you beat Nav at the cup."

Looking pleased, Josh asked, "What changed your mind?"

Will had no interest in going into details. He nodded pointedly at Josh's pancakes and advised, "Eat light. You've got a lot of jumping ahead." He left before Josh could make any reply. First off, he didn't care what Josh might have to say. The deal was set—that's all that mattered. Second, he knew that the minute he turned his back, Josh would shove that forkful of pancakes into his mouth anyway.

Will just hoped he wouldn't toss it back up during training.

Chapter 16

FRIENDSHIP ON THE ROCKS

K it spent the morning running through her dressage test on TK in the practice ring. She did it
over and over again, as if Elaine were with her, forcing her to start at the beginning every time she forgot
a move or made the wrong one. Spending time with
an imaginary Elaine wasn't Kit's idea of fun, but it
helped keep her alert.

"Working trot from H to A," she recited, guiding
TK just as she had guided her plastic horse around the
model ring a few nights ago. "Turn to center line, halt,
and we're done. We did it—woohoo!" She patted TK's
neck. "Good job, boy!" She laughed. "Good job, *me*!"

Buzzing with pride, Kit dismounted TK and
took a look around. She was alone in the ring. "Gotta
say," she told TK, "I thought there'd be more of a

feeling of triumph after that. Maybe it's just me, but I think there should be cupcakes or trumpets or"—she stroked TK's cheek—"maybe a best friend cheering for us?"

A horse's whinny drew her attention to the ring next to hers, where a younger student was finishing up jumping.

"Hm," Kit mused. "Maybe we're not done." She fixed TK with a mischievous look. "What do you think, boy? You up for trying something else today?"

Meanwhile, Rudy was fighting with paperwork at his desk in the tack room.

Paperwork was a truly frightening thing. No matter how much of it he did, signing reports here and ordering supplies there, his in-box always ended up with more paperwork in it than he started with. He was beginning to think that paperwork could actually breed, and that his in-box wasn't a piece of desk equipment but a paperwork nest in disguise.

A petite figure bustled into the room with a quick, "Good morning—just fetching my helmet. I'll see you out—" Sally stopped speaking, stopped moving. She stared at the doorway.

Rudy glanced up. "Something wrong, Miss Sally?"

Sally pinned him with a death glare. "You know exactly what's wrong," she said in a low voice. "The Rose Cottage good-luck horseshoe—what did you do with it?"

This was the moment that Rudy had been looking forward to all morning. He hadn't been sure exactly when Sally might stop by the tack room, but he knew she would. Now that the House Cup was getting close, she had begun taking daily rides with her Rose Cottage girls, probably to build up team spirit. And now that she had finally stepped into his domain, Rudy was ready for a little fun.

"I'm afraid I don't know what you're referring to," he said, his voice oozing with cowboy charm.

The expression on Sally's face was priceless. Her eyes were big, her lips pursed. Rudy thought she looked so cute that way, like a disgruntled sparrow when an uppity blue jay steals its worm. "It was here," she told him, pointing at the empty spot on the wall, "right here. A good-luck horseshoe. And it's been here for nearly twenty seasons—since *I* was a student!"

Rudy tipped his head to one side as if perplexed. "Huh. That's curious." He turned to Will. "Will, do you know anything about this?"

Will was busy cleaning tack in the corner. "No, sir," he replied.

"We don't know anything about it," Rudy told Sally.

The disgruntled sparrow turned into a feisty raven as Sally advanced on Rudy one slow step after another. "Your gee-whiz-aw-shucks cowboy act is not fooling me. This is *unacceptable*!" She narrowed her eyes in an attempt to look intimidating. Rudy just thought it made her look cuter. "Return my shoe, or you and your team will live to regret it!" Sally pantomimed *I am watching you*, and then, with a final glare and a harsh "Good day, Mr. Bridges," she left.

It was all Rudy could do not to bust a gut laughing.

Will looked at the empty space where the horseshoe had been. "Did you . . . ?"

Rudy would have liked to take Will in as a confidant—pranks were so much more fun when shared with other pranksters, and Will was a champ. But he decided to keep this prank between himself and Sally. "Maybe."

Will easily sensed the truth. "And Lady Covington thought I wasn't learning enough out here in the barn!"

An hour later, Kit was still in the practice ring working with TK. While he had taken a short rest, she had set up a simple jump course. Most of the jumps were only a few inches high, and some were just poles lying on the ground. Now she guided him through the course at a steady walk, using all of her willpower to stay calm and in control. She needed to communicate to TK that she was in charge, but also that he was safe under her charge. So far, it seemed to be working.

"Step one, two, three, four, jump," she recited, and TK walked over a pole on the ground. "Step one, two, three —"

TK balked and tried to veer sideways. Kit gently spoke his name and corrected his movements back toward the next jump. "Easy," she murmured, pouring all the calm energy she could into the word. "And . . . jump!"

TK awkwardly jumped over the only oxer in the course. It was about ten inches high, and he cleared it.

"All right!" Kit praised him. "Good boy!" She basked in the moment.

Anya had gone riding with Elaine, and as they returned, Anya stopped to watch Kit work with TK. "Look at that," she said to Elaine, who sat astride Thunder next to her.

Elaine watched TK clear the oxer. "Something you and I both mastered by the time we were six," she observed.

Anya didn't like how Elaine put Kit down. "But that's huge for her," she said, annoyed by how riders like Elaine just couldn't understand. Elaine had probably begun her career in competition as soon as she could walk, just like Anya had. Kit was a beginner.

When Kit suddenly noticed them watching, Anya smiled, hoping that her roommate would see how happy she was at TK's success. Instead, Kit's expression slid into disappointment, and she looked away.

Anya felt hollow.

"Well, I had fun," Elaine said, pulling Anya's attention back. "I hope we can do it again sometime."

Preoccupied, Anya nodded vaguely. "Yeah."

"Peaches and I are having a movie marathon tonight," Elaine went on. "All sports films, as inspiration." She smiled coyly. "I think you should join us."

Instead of answering, Anya looked out again at her roommate, who instantly looked away again. Was Kit mad at her? Of course she was, and why shouldn't she be? Anya had lied about her identity—there was no other way to phrase it. From Anya's point of view, she had been protecting herself, but from Kit's point of view, she had *lied*.

Anya decided she might as well accept Elaine's movie invitation. Kit probably wouldn't want to talk to her ever again. So the two girls rode back to the stables, removed their horses' tack, made the horses comfortable in their stalls, and then went to Rose Cottage.

Elaine plied Anya with questions the whole time, questions about living in the royal palace, about privileges she enjoyed in India—all the things Anya didn't want to talk about. She also suggested that Anya should pack some things, since Elaine had decided to turn the movie marathon into a sleepover. Anya wasn't thrilled by that. Watching movies was okay, but she still wanted to talk to Kit privately that evening . . .

if Kit would talk to her, that is. But she was trapped now. Worse, she had made the trap herself. And worse than *that*, she didn't know how to get out of it. Before she knew it, she was packing pajamas, her toiletries bag, and a few CDs into her tote while telling Elaine about, who else? Prince Harry. She found she couldn't stop. It was almost a relief, actually, to be talking freely about her home life for the first time since she'd come to Covington. "The gossip pages called my cousin a catch," she said, "except that he's a teenage boy, and, well, he *smells* like a teenage boy."

Elaine, comfortably perched on Kit's bed, listened in rapture. "And he's in Hong Kong?"

Anya nodded. "At the International School."

Kit had spent the last hour staying away from Anya and Elaine, then had taken care of TK's needs and headed to her room, where she'd hoped to spend a couple of hours relaxing. That, however, was not to be. For one thing, Elaine was there, sitting on her bed! And Anya appeared to be packing.

"Don't mind me," Kit said loudly upon entering the room.

Elaine slowly slid off her bed. "Anya was just regaling me with some fab tales from her incredibly glam life."

"Oh? I haven't heard many of those," Kit responded. To Anya she said, "Don't let me stop you, Your Highness."

The unpleasant vibes in the room were as oppressive as new riding boots, Kit decided.

"Right!" said Elaine. "Well, I'm going to go get the slumber party all set up. I'll see you later, Anya." She brushed past Kit and made her exit.

Chapter 17

NO GOOD-BYES

That was as much as Kit could tolerate. She went after Elaine and barged into her room. "You don't think I know what you're doing?"

"It matters here," Elaine said to Kit, as though she were talking to a child. "Who you align yourself with *matters.*"

"I don't care who I *align* myself with, Elaine," Kit retorted.

"Are you sure about that? Because there are advantages to having a friend like her. I mean, this kind of access is half the reason for coming to Covington."

"*Access?*" Kit felt her insides heave at the very idea of talking about people as convenient *things.*

Elaine obviously had no problem with that concept. "Who your friends are matters, would you not agree?" she asked in a reasonable tone.

Put that way, yes, Kit could agree. But there was much more to it than that. "Well . . . yeah . . ." she began thoughtfully.

Elaine didn't let her finish. "I guarantee you that, in what—six months? I'll be holidaying in luxury at some Patel family compound. If you were smart, you'd get back in her good books, too."

Outside Elaine's door, Anya had been listening in on Kit and Elaine's entire conversation. It was just as she had feared: now that her secret was out, Covington might as well be the palace. She turned and rushed away, because she had heard enough to know that it was time to go.

Kit was furious with Elaine for implying that Kit would act out of—or even have—ulterior motives. "I don't care about that! Anya's my friend because she's my friend!"

Elaine shook her head. "Well, remind me to never invite you onto the debating team."

"I owe her an apology. And not Princess Anya but . . . *Anya*." Kit left, slamming the door behind her. She immediately started back down the empty hallway to her and Anya's room, but then she paused. *I'm too riled up right now to apologize properly*, she thought. *I need to settle down first.*

She headed downstairs and, finding the Rose Cottage common room empty, paced its length a few times. *Not helping!* she thought, so she went out the back door and sat in the small courtyard, hoping that some fresh night air would slow her racing heart.

All I want from Anya is friendship, she thought. *Doesn't she know that by now? Haven't I proven that? I don't care if she's got forty-seven gold crowns and twenty pairs of magic princess slippers! I like her because she's a nice person!* With a growl, she leaped to her feet and took a step to the door. *Nope, nope, nope, you're still angry, Bridges. Sit back down and chill.*

She did, but as the seconds ticked by and turned into minutes, she remained angry. Why? Anya had only protected herself; Kit could see that now. Elaine stood as a glaring example of exactly what Anya had been protecting herself *from*.

Thinking about defense mechanisms reminded her of Charlie, the friend she had left behind in Montana when she had moved to England. Charlie's family wasn't well off. They lived in a small house with a crooked front door and never enough firewood during the winter. When Charlie had joined Kit for shopping sprees at the thrift store in town, she always knew that Charlie's purchases were out of need, whereas hers were for style. But they never talked about that, in part because Kit rarely had the opportunity to call him anymore. And furthermore, she knew he was embarrassed about it, because in the sixth grade his whole face had gone bright red when Joey McGillis teased him loudly about his threadbare pants. Kit had wanted to punch Joey square in the face, but seeing how uncomfortable Charlie was made her realize that violence toward others wasn't what he needed from her. He needed a friend. And come to think of it, so did Anya. She and Charlie may have been on opposite ends of the socioeconomic spectrum, but everyone had struggles and needed someone by their side. She wanted to be that, for both of them.

She took out her phone. It was still daytime back in Montana, so she texted, *Hey, creep! Whassup?*

Hi! came a return text right away. *In class, u clown. Algebra barf. Hey r u*

Kit waited for the rest, then burst out laughing. *He got caught texting in class!* she thought, and laughed harder. *I'd better text him an apology later, since it's my fault. I hope he doesn't get detention!*

She felt much better, though, just from that goofy exchange and a dose of laughter. *It's time,* she thought. It was time to face Anya.

When she got to their room, it was empty. Not just empty of Anya, but of all her belongings, too. Her nightstand and dressing table were cleared off, her work desk empty of everything but the lamp and vase of flowers. Kit ran to Anya's wardrobe and yanked the doors open — totally empty.

"Oh, no," Kit murmured. "No, no, no, no . . ." She bolted out of Rose Cottage and headed to the practice ring, where she knew Josh and Will were training for the cup. She didn't particularly want to see Will. Josh was her target.

As she approached the ring, she heard a mild argument in progress.

"You signaled him too early," Will was saying. "Back to the start."

"Oh, come on, man," complained Josh, sitting astride his chestnut gelding, Whistler.

"This is for the cup, mate!" Will insisted. "Back to the start!" Josh grumbled but obeyed, trotting Whistler back to the end of the ring as Will added, "Remember, your heels are your anchor, your legs are the guardrail, and the engine's in the back."

"Okay, okay! You drive a hard bargain."

"And you need to ride harder."

Josh guided Whistler over the jump again. Even Kit could see Will's frown.

"Look, I'll do better tomorrow," Josh said, sounding tired.

Will pointed at the jump. "There's still an hour to curfew."

"Hey!" Kit called to Josh before the boys could get into a real argument. "Have you seen your pretend girlfriend?"

"Anya?" Josh asked. "Uh, no. I've been in here for what feels like decades."

Will's eyes narrowed. "Hey!" he barked, and again pointed at the jump. "Go!"

With a sigh, Josh said, "Sorry," to Kit and turned Whistler once again to the far end of the ring.

So much for that idea, Kit thought. *So where could Anya be? It hasn't been that long. She must have packed her stuff in, like, five seconds, so she's still got to be here somewh* . . . Her thoughts trailed off as she saw her answer, right in front of her at the entrance to Covington's main building. A chauffeur was placing what looked to be the last bag of several into a limousine's trunk. "Wait," she said, then louder, "Wait!"

Anya appeared and got into the limo's backseat.

"Anya!" Kit yelled. *"Anya!"* She ran for the limo, waving her arms. *"Wait!"*

Did Anya hear her? It didn't matter. The limo drove away.

Chapter 18

THE CURSE OF THE MISSING HORSESHOE

It was the big day — the day of the Covington House Cup!

Kit stood in the tack room with all the other Rose Cottage girls. They were dressed in their competition uniforms, their boots polished, makeup perfect, teeth cleaned, and all of them completely demoralized.

Anya, one of their best riders, was gone. She had left school.

For Kit, this wasn't just a competition problem but a personal disaster. She wanted to be doing what Anya always did when she was upset — hiding in bed under the covers. But her team needed her, and although her abilities weren't as honed as those of her peers, she was ready to try her hardest.

Sally Warrington was giving a pep talk. "Now more than ever, we have got to take that cup!" she said. "We need to give Juniper Cottage a kick in the backside, is that clear?"

Everyone nodded, but they should have been cheering or something, shouldn't they? The news about Anya was a downer, yes, but as Kit glanced around, she noticed that several girls looked more than upset or dismayed. Several seemed on edge, as if they knew something terrible was about to happen. The feeling in the room was hardly one of energetic team spirit, that was for sure. What was going on?

Sally pulled back a bit. "No pressure, though," she said meekly. "We won't worry about Anya, not today, all right? She's just fine. She's chosen to leave Covington. It's that simple. We'll miss her, of course, but we've got a team of very strong riders!"

"For the most part," Elaine muttered, glancing at Kit.

"That's enough, Elaine," said Sally. "Now, girls, are we confident?"

All Kit could muster was a smile. With what looked like brute determination alone, Elaine and

Peaches said, "Yes," with about, maybe, twenty-percent effort. The rest of the girls just stood there.

Meanwhile, at the other end of the stables, Rudy was giving a pep talk to the Juniper Cottage boys. "Whose turn is it to take home the Covington House Cup?"

"Juniper Cottage!" all the boys roared back together. Even with Will out of the competition, they were pumped.

"Are we confident?" Rudy shouted.

"Yes! We! Are!" they answered, Josh and Nav exchanging high fives with each word.

Rudy continued, "You're riding for league standing against students from all across the U.K.! The house with the highest points takes home the Covington House Cup!" Rudy lowered his voice: "Which I hear is a bit of a big deal." With a mischievous competitive gleam in his eye, he finished, "Let's take it back from those girls, huh? Huddle up!"

Rudy held out his hand, and all the boys stacked their hands on his one by one. They leaned in, vibrating with energy, as Rudy counted, "One! Two! Three!"

"*Juniper Cottage!*" they shouted as all hands flew upward.

"Take 'em down!" Rudy cried, and the boys clapped and stomped. They were ready, all right.

In the tack room, the funereal silence was broken by Sally's desperate cry of "The boys are going down!"

One of the Rose Cottage girls suddenly slapped a hand over her mouth and rushed out of the room.

"Oh!" said Sally. "Oh, dear. What in the world is happening?"

Elaine whipped a surgical mask from her pocket and put it on her face. "*You!*" She turned to Peaches. "I told you not to bring that horrid smoked salmon into the cottage!" She scrutinized the group. "Who else ate the fish?"

Kit watched as four hesitant hands went up. Yup, those were the same girls who looked unusually on edge. Several of the other girls gasped as the situation became clear.

Peaches just shrugged. "I ate it, and I'm fine."

Elaine was livid. "Why a person would bring

room-temperature *fish* into our cottage on *competition eve* is simply beyond me!"

No one knew quite what to do until Sally said in a low, mysterious tone, "This is surely the curse of the missing horseshoe." She stared at an empty spot on the wall. Kit recalled that a horseshoe had hung there, but it wasn't there now. Why was it gone? "It happened once before when I was in Fifth Form," Sally went on as if in answer to Kit's unspoken question. "It was an unmitigated disaster. Joanie got kicked in the leg, Bet's horse escaped and was gone the whole day, and my horse, Sadie"—the memory of Sadie made Sally pause to smile lovingly, but then she launched back into her tale—"she stopped right before the jump, and I continued flying over, and I fell in a heap and chipped a tooth."

Elaine pulled Sally back to reality. "Respectfully, Miss Warrington," she said through her mask, "it's a horseshoe."

Two more girls suddenly stumbled for the door, doubled over, hands to mouths.

"Oh, dear!" Sally despaired. "Oh, no!"

It was at this point that Elaine pulled a paper

from her pocket, stating firmly, "We'll just have to dip into our list of reserve riders."

"Yes!" Sally took the list like a drowning person grabbing a life preserver. "Who do we have? Who else can do the jumpers?" She fought with the paper until it was properly right-side up. "Um, Kiki Welch?" she read out.

Kit shook her head *no* to indicate that Kiki must have eaten the fish. She'd been the first girl to leave.

"No?" said Sally. "Uh, Jilly. Jilly Jones?"

Also gone.

Sally muttered, "Poor Jilly," and desperately went back to the list. "Babe Scarrow?"

Right on cue, Babe grabbed a nearby trash can and, lowering her head over it, lunged out of the room.

As Sally looked at a loss, Elaine took charge. "That leaves us with you, Peaches. Tack up for the jumper course."

Peaches's body went rigid. "You know I only do dressage," she said. "I'm afraid of heights!"

Kit had seen and heard enough. This clown show had to be set right somehow. So she took a deep breath and said, "I'll do it!" When nobody said anything, Kit thought, *They don't think I'm capable. They don't trust me.*

Well, I'll show them! "I've been practicing," she told them. "You know I have. It's worth a shot, right?"

"Well," Sally said, looking relieved, "it's worth a thought, certainly."

Elaine was right on cue. "Respectfully, Miss Warrington, it's worth nothing. I've been training Kit—I should know. She's simply not ready."

Kit wanted to protest, but Elaine charged ahead. "Peaches, you are going to eat your fear. Get yourself sorted."

Peaches gave Elaine a timid, pathetic look.

"Now!"

Peaches scuttled away to get ready.

Sally said to Kit, "It seems today's not the day to risk it, I'm afraid. I'm sorry, Kit."

Kit tried to pretend that it didn't bother her, but it did. It bothered her a lot.

Will felt shattered, as if he were walking around in pieces held together in human form by a hasty tape job. He should be riding today! Instead, his riding skills were going to waste while he handed out programs. He was despondent. And angry.

Oh, yes, very angry.

"Hey," came a familiar voice as Rudy walked into Covington's indoor competition ring. "Where were you? You missed my stirring and brilliant pep talk."

Will, up in the spectator bleachers, looked down at his riding instructor. "They've got me ushering."

"You're still part of my team. We could have used your smiling face in there."

Will gave him a you've-got-to-be-joking expression.

"Hmm, well, your *could*-be-smiling face?" Rudy said. "Your *occasionally* smiling face?"

At this point, Will was positively scowling. "Yep, well, this is an important job," he said scornfully. He held up one of the House Cup program sheets that he was supposed to fold and drape across the back of each spectator chair. "I've got to get the corners straight." He sloppily folded the sheet in half to demonstrate.

"I'm sorry you're not riding today," Rudy told him sincerely. "I wish you were. But you'll still get your scores for the all-schools league. Just not today."

Will lost it. "Right! Yeah! Because riding alone

for the judges on the makeup day is just as much fun, isn't it?"

"You'd rather ride in front of the crowd," said Rudy. It wasn't a question.

"Yeah!" said Will. "The horses get excited! And everyone's cheering! And competing is just"—he searched through his angry thoughts to find the right words—"a thrill! And when do well, it *matters*! And everyone *sees* that it matters!"

There was so much more to it than that, but Will clamped his jaws shut and turned away. Nobody could understand how important it was to him to be out there, contributing his hard-earned talents to the team and competing as a part of something so grand and majestic. Winning was great, it always was, but that wasn't the critical part. The critical part was that amazing partnership between human and beast, working together within a team to achieve great things. It mattered. It really, really did.

It mattered to *him*.

Kit gripped TK's brush and lovingly ran it through his long silky tail. She wanted him to look his best for their dressage test. As she moved the brush along, she gave him a blow-by-blow of that morning's embarrassing pep talk.

"Miss Warrington was about to let us compete, and then Elaine had to jump right in there with *Respectfully, Miss Warrington*. She wouldn't even give me a chance!"

TK blew hard through his nose — his version of a big sigh of understanding and camaraderie.

Kit laughed. "I hear you. Well, we'll just have to go and kill it in the dressage ring."

TK nodded.

"Just really crush it!" Kit continued, amused as TK nodded again. *At least* he *agrees with me,* she thought.

Nav approached the stall, dressed in a competition uniform.

"Whoa." Kit scanned him up and down, especially noting his white silk tie. "You look super swag."

Nav gave her one of his patented suave smiles. "I came to wish you all the best in the field today," he said graciously.

"You, too," said Kit. "And thank you so much. I couldn't have done it without you."

Nav maintained his smile, but there was a pinch of confusion in it now.

"The sticky notes," Kit reminded him. "They made all the difference."

"Sticky notes?" He seemed to think it over. "What notes?"

Before Kit could answer, the Covington House Cup announcer said over the stable speakers, "All first-round dressage competitors to the ring."

Then "You're joking, right?" she continued to Nav. "Is it all part of the secret admir—uhh . . ." Kit suddenly understood. Whatever was going on, Nav was *not* the sticky-note writer, which meant that he was not her secret admirer, as she had thought. Quickly she covered her almost-blunder with "Uh, I mean, the whole secret-*adviser*-dude thing?"

Nav chuckled at her stumbled words, probably thinking that she was just nervous about competing. "Concentrate on your ride," he said. "Go be stellar." Then he flashed his perfect smile one more time and left.

Kit looked at TK. "If he's not my note writer, then who is?"

If TK could have shrugged, he probably would have.

The central corridor of Covington's main building was serving as the welcoming point for family members of the House Cup competitors. A blue-and-gold banner declaring COVINGTON HOUSE CUP hung over the entryway. Beyond it, a lavish refreshment table offered the finest teas and nibbles from polished silver urns and trays, while several smaller tables scattered here and there offered other tasty tidbits. The floor sparkled, the woodwork gleamed, and even the flower displays were fuller and brighter than usual. Parents and family members meandered about, nibbling and admiring the artwork.

This was Lady Covington's territory. Here she greeted each family as they arrived, offering the kind of formal chitchat expected at an elite institution such as Covington. Dressed in a fine black skirt suit, she was currently speaking to one of the school's most prestigious donors. "Ah, Mr. Jasper-Eton. It's lovely to see you, and I love your tie. You must have a look at our new media room on your way out to the grounds. Thank you so much for making that happen." She shook his hand gratefully.

As Mr. Jasper-Eton left, a Scottish-accented voice called out, "Lady Covington!"

An older man and woman stalked toward her. The man did not look happy, so the headmistress turned her charm factor up to ten. "Ah, Mr. Chatfield!" She held out her hand to him.

Mr. Chatfield did not take the offered hand. Instead he grumbled, "Our request for the front row was submitted eons ago." As he spoke, his voice grew louder and louder until he was yelling. "Our Nelly deserves to see her parents—who have traveled all the way from Fife—*in the front row*!"

"Of course she does," Lady Covington heartily agreed, and she held up her copy of the seating chart. "And there you are, there, right there," and she pointed to two seats in the front row.

But now Mr. Chatfield was glaring at a newcomer who wanted Lady Covington's attention. "Señora Covington!" shouted the newcomer in a heavy Spanish accent.

Lady Covington recognized Nav's mother, Luciana, a stern woman who was towing not only her silent husband but several little Andradas of varying ages. "Hello, Mrs. Andrada—"

"This is unbelievable! You have seated me in the back row with the pigeons!"

Lady Covington again consulted her seating chart. "Mrs. Andrada, see? You're right there in the front row."

"No!" Mrs. Andrada cried out in a voice that could shatter glass. "I'm not. I'm with the pigeons!" Her voice suddenly went low and dangerous. "The competition is about to begin, and if I miss my Navarro's round due to the utter incompetence of your little operation here . . ." From that point, she lapsed into Spanish, leaving Lady Covington unable to help her at all.

Mr. Chatfield decided to join in with "I'm with her!" as Mrs. Andrada started naming off her children one by one, pointing them out and, Lady Covington guessed, threatening to enroll them in schools other than Covington when they came of age.

With all the English grace and manners she could muster, the headmistress proceeded to calm her patrons down.

The commotion ten minutes later in the viewing stands was nothing short of comical, with rich, well-dressed people shuffling back and forth, trying to find their assigned seats. But no matter how many times they checked their seating charts, they could not match the assignments up with the actual seat labels. They pushed around one another in the narrow aisles, sitting down with relief and then getting caught up in arguments when someone else claimed the same seat. They dropped jeweled handbags and expensive hats in the muddle and stepped on one another's stylish shoes. The continuous muttered chorus of "Excuse me," "Ouch!" and "That's my chair!" grew gradually louder and louder.

Nav gazed at the scene, enjoying every second of parental chaos. He pulled out his mobile phone and started to record the whole thing, snickering in delight. When Will walked up, wondering what was going on, Nav laughed, "Look at my mother!" Imitating her, he said, "It is simply ridiculous that I am not in the *VIP section* of the *VIP section* next to the *VIPs*!" He kept recording, adding, "Before today, the woman didn't even know what a back row was!"

Will felt his stomach do a threatening flip-flop. He pulled out his copy of the master seating chart and checked it. Everything looked right to him. Then Nav's words *back row* echoed in his head. With a sinking sensation, he turned the seating chart upside down—*that* was the way it was supposed to be! He had labeled all the seats *backward*!

"Uh-oh," he said.

Chapter 19

IT ONLY GETS WORSE FROM HERE

W hat's with all the drama?" asked Josh as he joined them.

"Ask Will," Nav said, his evil grin widening. He patted Will's back. "Best of luck with that mess. I've got a competition to win."

"Uh-oh," Will said again.

"Hey, does he know about our bet, dude?" Josh asked. "Because I just cannot wait to beat him and get that nice room for myself."

Will didn't care about that. All he could focus on was Sally Warrington heading his way, angrily waving at him. "Not now, Josh," he said, and dashed away.

"I've already voodooed Nav," Josh called after him, "and performed my never-fail precompetition ritual. Tune in, bro!"

The next half hour was an uncomfortable mixture of ego soothing, official apologies, and plenty of bowing and scraping, but eventually Lady Covington got all the family members, sponsors, and spectators seated correctly in the bleachers. She herself then took a seat up in the back row "with the pigeons," as Mrs. Andrada had put it.

Finally, it was time. The event began.

"Riding for Rose Cottage, Elaine Wiltshire," droned the House Cup announcer over the speakers.

Elaine guided her chestnut gelding, Thunder, over the jumps, sitting tall and confident in the saddle while Thunder cantered with controlled precision up and over, up and over, jump after jump. Elaine made no mistakes, and Thunder performed beautifully, receiving a perfect score.

Outside, Nav was walking Prince around the lawn. Standing and waiting were not skills that either Nav or his mount were particularly good at, so they waited their turn at a lazy walk, breathing in the cool countryside air before having to face the harsh lights and tension of the ring.

"Hey!" said Josh, joining them. "You seen Kit, buddy?"

"Sure," Nav replied distractedly. "In the stables." He was deep in his mental preparations for the competition, and he didn't like being disturbed. But Josh did seem concerned about something.

"Coolness," Josh said. "I'm just kind of worried about him — you know, our friend."

"Who?" asked Nav. "Mr. Bridges?"

"No, Will. It's just, he's so bummed about not being able to ride in the cup, and now he's going to catch it for the whole seating catastrophe thing, too. And I just think he could use a little cheering up, right? And Kit, being such a decent person and all, she's going to be all over making him feel better. Life, huh?" He smiled. "Good luck today. You know, big day." He cast his eye on Prince. "Looks good." He gave Nav a final nod and left.

Nav frowned. He knew very well that Josh was trying to unsettle him just before his ride. How typical. And how childish, to try to beat your competition by rattling their nerves seconds before they perform. Annoying, that's what it was. Disgusting, really.

He heard his name announced, so he walked Prince into the ring. As he began the course, he realized that he did feel a bit guilty. Will really was taking a lot of punishment this term, and a lot of it had been for his sake. Nav wondered if he'd been fair to Will lately.

The first jump seemed to come out of nowhere. Nav snapped back to reality, guiding Prince up and over. But Prince balked as he approached the second jump, and his back hooves brushed the pole as he went over. The next few jumps were clean, and Nav thought all would be well until, at the very last jump, he glanced into the stands and locked eyes with Josh for the fleetest second. What was it Josh had said, about Kit comforting Will? Wait, did that mean Kit liked Will? But *he* liked Kit! Jealousy shot through Nav like a lightning bolt, and Prince, instantly detecting his rider's unease, knocked down the final jump.

The announcer said, "I'm afraid Nav Andrada has accumulated four faults. That will cost his standing."

Struggling to keep raw fury from showing on his face, Nav rode Prince out of the ring, deliberately looking away from the people in the stands. He could feel the disappointment from Lady Covington and the sympathy from Rudy Bridges. He presumed that Josh was grinning.

The reception hallway of Covington's main building was empty now, as everyone had gone to watch the competition. Only a few students milled around, stationed there to attend to anyone who might happen by.

Peaches wandered into the long empty space, wondering why she was there. She was holding her saddle, but there weren't any horses around. And was *she* wobbling or was everything *else* wobbling? It was all quite mysterious. So she just kept walking.

Elaine rushed up to her, looking frenzied, as though she had been looking everywhere. "Peaches! You're going the wrong way!" Peaches didn't stop, forcing Elaine to physically block her path. "If you need to go to the toilet, you should have thought about that earlier. Oh"—Elaine took a good look at her lackey—"you look . . . flushed."

That was one way to put it. Peaches's cheeks were red with fever, her eyes half-lidded, her skin slick with sweat.

"In fact," Elaine said, "you look rather like a piece of smoked salmon."

In a slow, thick voice, Peaches insisted, "I—I feel absolutely ace!"

"Oh, Peaches . . ."

"You were right. . . ." Peaches moaned before she slowly crumpled to the floor, dropping her saddle to clutch at her stomach. "It was the fish. . . ."

At that precise moment, Elaine's view of the world changed. Her logical, disciplined, ever-rational mind suddenly accepted the illogical, the undisciplined, and the irrational. Why? Because everything was going wrong for Rose Cottage, and it had been going wrong ever since Sally noticed the missing Rose Cottage good-luck horseshoe.

"I believe," she found herself muttering. "I believe." She started to run back outside, declaring, "I believe in the curse!"

In the tack room, Will was trying to defend himself. Sally had finally cornered him and dragged him to see Rudy. "I didn't do it on purpose!" Will told Rudy. "Honestly! The seating chart was the wrong way around!"

"Lady Covington was not pleased," Sally added.

Rudy paused in his pacing. "You don't say."

Sally looked at Rudy imploringly. "What do we do? She'll want an explanation for what happened."

"I just want to go hide in my room and give her some time to calm down," said Will. "I messed up— again. That's all there is to it. That's all I know how to do, apparently."

Rudy looked him straight in the eye and made a decision. "That's not true. Tack up."

Both Will and Sally spoke at the same time: "*What?*"

"You heard me."

"But Lady Covington said—"

"I am the stable master," Rudy said, cutting Will off, "and I am telling you to tack up and get out there."

Unable to believe his ears, Will obeyed as the House Cup announcer said over the speaker, "Katherine Bridges, please report to the dressage ring."

Kit led TK out of his stall. She was ready, TK was ready, everything was ready! "We're good," she told her horse as they headed for the dressage ring. "We've got this. If you nail it, I promise you, like, a thousand carrots!"

TK seemed to like that idea. He whuffled and bumped her shoulder with his nose.

Oh, good, he's happy! Kit thought. *We are going to really do this right, and Lady Covington will be so pleased, and everything will be great!*

Just then, Elaine ran into the stable. "You'll have to do dressage later," she panted. "You're up right now. For jumping."

A million different responses collided in Kit's mind, but only one word made it out of her mouth: *"What?"*

Instead of offering encouragement, Elaine merely said, "I know. Not ideal." And she rushed back out, leaving Kit with her jaw hanging.

Chapter 20

"IT WAS JUST A JOKE"

Riding for Juniper Cottage," said the House Cup announcer, "Josh Luders and Whistler."

Josh rode Whistler out into the ring. Centering his mind, he signaled Whistler to start, and the round began. Up and over, up and over poles of different bright color combinations, Josh urged his mount to keep a steady pace and an even steadier mind. He was completely focused on each obstacle as it came, maintaining energy while keeping Whistler in control. The gelding attentively heeded his rider's signals, and at the end of their round, the announcer said, "A clear ride for Josh Luders. Nicely done!"

Josh saw the scoreboard and gave Whistler a pat on the neck. "Yyyyes!"

As he rode past the stands and out of the ring, Nav was there to say, "Good show," as he went by.

"Thanks, dude," Josh replied, ignoring the disappointment on Nav's face. All he cared about was that new dorm room he was going to get. No more awful roommate, either—score!

In the stable, Kit was trying to come to grips with her future, specifically, the next ten minutes or so.

First off, she had to tack up TK all over again. He was wearing a dressage saddle, which was designed with a deep seat to keep the rider sitting with a very straight back and even straighter legs. Now she had to put a jump saddle on him, which was designed to keep the rider's legs bent so that they could lift themselves up out of the shallower seat over jumps. TK accepted all of Kit's fussing and even let her babble at him at ten thousand miles an hour as she worked.

"I cannot believe that I'm going to jump! It's a good thing I don't have too much time to think about it, because the Best/Worst game could go on for hours. Like, I could start you off too fast and mess up the first jump, and that would just ruin it right off the bat, right? Or a bee could fly into your ear, or you could throw a shoe, or I could get so nervous that I throw up in front of the whole school. But I think the very worst of the worst has to be the girth going loose and me simply falling out of the saddle like a sack of potatoes. That would be the worst, right?" She said this as she tightened the girth a second time, making sure the jump saddle was secure but not too tight around TK's barrel. "There! I think that's it, boy. We're ready!" She petted TK's nose. "As ready as we're going to get, anyway."

Her eye caught a glimpse of yellow on top of the new saddle. Peering closer, Kit saw that it was a yellow sticky note that read, *I BELIEVE in you!* She peeled the note free and looked around, unable to see anyone who might have left it. So she walked around TK to check his other side.

Will stood there, looking handsome indeed in a crisp competition uniform.

"These were you?" Kit asked, holding up the note, dumbfounded.

"Maybe," Will answered nervously. "Is . . . is that a good thing?"

Was it a good thing? Kit had only one answer to that. She ran to him and kissed him on the cheek. "So good!"

Will blushed. "I . . . I, um . . . I didn't think you'd ever forgive me, you know, after the whole Guy thing."

"Well, I do. And I'm so glad for you, that you get to ride today!" Kit looked up at him and got lost in his smile. Words flitted through her mind, words that were so corny and yet so accurate: Will's eyes were *soulful*, his smile *dazzling*, his eyebrows so *expressive*! She was sure she was blushing, too.

"William Palmerston to the ring," said the House Cup announcer over the speaker. "William Palmerston."

Will tore his eyes from Kit as he heard his name. "That's me."

"Yes, it is." Kit scrambled for something meaningful to say. "Um, break a leg!"

One of Will's very expressive eyebrows quirked. "Yeah, we don't say that."

Oh, right, Kit thought. *That's theater. Then how about this?* "You're going to be amazing out there. You always are." She clutched the yellow sticky note as

Will hurried away. Kit watched him go. She so wished she could watch his round, but it was time to get ready for her own!

Will entered the ring astride Wayne—Sir Gawain, his bay gelding. Wayne was in fine spirits, as he usually was. Will loved the horse for his steady yet competitive disposition. He could feel Wayne quiver beneath him in excitement. This is what Will had tried to describe to Rudy Bridges earlier. There was nothing like riding Wayne in a competition, where he and the horse exchanged energy and supported each other in their quest for a common goal. It was the best feeling in the world to know that their efforts were being observed and appreciated, that all the hard work had a definite reason and outcome. It was the only time Will felt truly *alive*.

As usual, he rode the course faster than any other student. He and Wayne both preferred to match accuracy with speed. Wayne cleared jump after jump, listening to the words and body signals that Will gave him: turn this way, speed up, slow down, prepare, and jump! Will accepted the applause of his fellow classmates as he rode, knowing that Wayne, in his own way, ate up the sounds of approval, too, converting them into even more competitive energy.

"Will Palmerston and Sir Gawain really put on some speed today," the announcer commented as horse and rider approached the final jump. Will signaled, Wayne responded, and horse and rider flew like birds for a moment, effortlessly clearing the poles and making a clean landing, both of them drinking in the applause as it rose for the final and loudest time. Wayne pranced with pride as Will rode him out of the ring, and Will couldn't help but grin.

"Best time yet," Rudy praised him as he rode up. "Way to go."

Will reined Wayne in for a quick moment. "Thanks," he said. "And thanks for letting me—"

"Yeah, speaking of that—lie low. You did good, but we still have a dragon lady to manage." Rudy's eyes flicked upward, indicating Lady Covington up in the back row. She was staring at Will with that blank expression she often used, the one that made it impossible to tell what she was thinking. Will knew that Rudy had stuck his neck out on his behalf, so he gave the headmistress a smile, hoping that would be taken as a polite gesture on his part, and rode Wayne back into the stables.

When Will was gone, Josh gave Nav a friendly smack on the arm. "Brah killed it! Man, he beat us both! Hey, it's a good thing he's in the same house, though. Kind of takes the sting out of coming in third place, eh?"

Nav clenched his jaws but said nothing.

The loudspeaker crackled to life, and the House Cup announcer said, "Next, Katherine Bridges will be riding TK on behalf of Rose Cottage."

Kit rode TK into the ring, her heart pounding so hard that she could feel it in her toes. She felt so grateful when her dad jumped into the ring and ran over to her. "I need the Ugly Brooch!" she whispered to him.

"Oh, jeez, I wish I had thought of it," Rudy said, pulling something out of his coat pocket. It was the brooch. He smiled as he handed it to her.

"You knew." Kit wanted to hug him so badly, but now wasn't the time. She accepted the brooch and slipped it into her pocket. "You knew I'd need it."

"Well," said Rudy, "I've known you for a long time."

Elaine was there, as well, to deliver some final advice. "Head up. Core tight. Don't mess up. Don't let the curse of the horseshoe get to you. You need to make *every* jump."

Right. Thanks a lot, Elaine, Kit thought, more terrified now than she had been before.

Elaine seemed to notice. "You'll be fine. You're Elaine-trained. Surely some of it stuck." She offered Kit a genuine smile.

Kit couldn't remember ever seeing a genuine smile on Elaine's face before. *Well, what do you know! Maybe she really is trying to help after all!*

Kit took a deep breath. Father and trainer stepped away.

Now it was all up to Kit.

She urged TK into a slow trot and took him around the ring, just to get them both settled and ready. TK's gait remained smooth as she turned him left to begin the approach to the first jump. It was just a tiny thing, one pole elevated no more than six inches off the ground. TK trotted steadily up to it.

And stopped dead.

Kit's first reaction was panic, but she tamped it down and firmly signaled TK to proceed. Instead, TK stepped backward, tossing his head in agitation. She tried to turn him back to it, and he turned halfway around, then sidestepped again.

"Come on, TK," Kit pleaded softly, "not now. This isn't hip-hop class."

The audience was silent as Kit struggled with TK. She couldn't stop him from weaving in place one way, then the other, as if he couldn't decide which way to turn. *You're not supposed to turn at all!* she thought-screamed at him. *Move! Forward!*

He stepped backward.

"Come on, buddy, enough already!" she hissed. *Don't you care at all?* she thought. *Lady Covington is watching us! Elaine is watching us! EVERYBODY is watching us, and you're acting like you've never done this before! If we don't get this right, you'll be sent away! Have you forgotten about that?*

The buzzer sounded, indicating that they should begin the course or forfeit. Kit looked at her dad for help. He could do nothing, of course, and he glanced worriedly over at Will, who appeared mortified by Kit's dilemma.

When TK reared up, Kit knew she was in deep trouble. She tried to center her mind so that TK would feel her confidence and respond, but for all of her effort, the only thing she managed to conjure up was the image of a very unhappy Lady Covington. It hardly inspired confidence. "Come on, TK!" she whined, feeling more helpless than she ever had in her life.

TK refused to move.

Now Kit got mad. She had worked far too hard for everything to end like this. She had put up with TK's nonsense, Elaine's attitude, everybody's doubts, and Lady Covington's threats. Well, enough was enough! She dismounted and told the crowd, "I need a minute!" *Is that even in the rules?* she wondered briefly, but it was too late now if it wasn't.

She faced TK square on. "We are doing it again, and we are going to go over that jump!"

TK tossed his head as if to say, "Nope, not gonna."

"Come on, buddy, there's no getting out of this."

He tossed his head again.

"No!" Kit snapped. "Don't you dare try to argue with me! We are doing this!"

Kit jumped at the sound of Rudy's voice: "It's all right, kid. You tried! Just bring him in!"

Throughout Kit's life, there had been times when she knew she'd crossed over the Big Line — like the time she had taken her sixth-year birthday cake out of its hiding place and eaten the entire thing all by herself in her bedroom just before dinner, or the time she had "borrowed" her dad's truck (without a license) and driven herself and Charlie to the thrift store to go shopping when she was supposed to be cleaning her room instead. Those mistakes had gotten her in lots of trouble, but this — this entire situation would get her into more trouble than she could imagine if TK didn't cooperate. Everything that mattered to Kit was on the line, and she was screwing it up! *No, not me*, she thought angrily. *It's TK's fault! He won't listen to me!*

"No!" she told her dad, in front of the entire audience. "This is *so* not over!"

Of all the voices to invade her mind at that moment, it was Elaine's. She had once advised Kit that TK was an unusually delicate horse by nature. "That means that you have to stay calm and relaxed at all times. If you're not calm, he won't be, either."

Okay. Okay. I'm calm. I'm calm. Kit took a deep breath and looked into TK's big, dark eyes. Trying not to shake so hard, she approached TK's side so that she could mount him again.

TK reared high, his hooves flailing through the air with enough power to kill her if they struck. Everyone in the audience gasped as Kit lurched back in fear. She ended up tripping over her own feet, and TK let out a shrill whinny and galloped off to the far end of the ring.

The audience fell silent while Rudy and Will ran out into the ring and gently helped Kit back to her feet. She tried not to cry, but the minute she looked into Will's grief-stricken face, she felt the waterworks begin. She hid her face in her dad's chest and cried.

"What happened out there?"

Kit stood before TK in his stall. After leaving the competition ring and returning to the stables, she had asked Will and her father if she could be alone for a while. They had understood and left. Now she confronted TK and, whether it made sense or not, furiously tore into him, more to relieve her own tensions than to accomplish anything. TK just stood there, pointedly facing away from her.

"We practiced! I got on a horse! That was impossible just a few weeks ago! My cottage lost the whole thing to the boys! And you! *You!* What *was* that? Elaine can take that up with *you!*"

TK shook his head and tried to nuzzle her.

"No," Kit said. "Don't you dare try to talk to me right now! I'm too mad!" She paused. "Sometimes you *really are a donkey*!"

Kit slid TK's stall door shut and left.

In the tack room, Rudy was tidying up, more in an effort to feel like he could help put his kid's world back in order than to actually accomplish anything. The students would come in on their own time and clean their own saddles, each of which sat on a saddle stand in a row that spanned the entire room. Bridles and other tack hung on pegs or were scattered across various tabletops.

Rudy folded up some of the house banners and was about to deposit them into a bin for washing when he saw a terrible sight: Sally Warrington, look-ing feverish and exhausted, slumped on the floor in a corner.

"You don't look so hot," he said. "You okay?"

"Certainly," Sally slurred back, waving a hand at him. "Nothing to fret about."

Rudy wasn't so sure about that. "Why don't you let me help you up—?"

"Not until you give me the horseshoe," she said sharply.

"What?"

"I've got half the girls of Rose Cottage cramming the toilets, and I can't . . ." She blinked very slowly. "I can't seem to move. So unless you want to play nurse-maid . . ."

Rudy gave in. The poor woman was so sick that he didn't have the heart to tease her a second longer. He reached up to a high shelf and took the horseshoe down. "It was just a joke," he said, handing it out to her. "I'm sorry. Truly."

Sally grabbed for it. The second she touched it, her eyes cleared and she managed to stand up. Rudy thought he might be witnessing a miracle.

"I would watch yourself, Mr. Bridges," Sally warned him, clutching her beloved lucky horseshoe in her hands. "And stay away from the fish."

She marched out, her movements a little unsteady, but her head held high. Rudy watched her, feeling bad about all the trouble his little joke had caused. He hoped Sally would give him an opportunity to make it up to her.

Chapter 21

THE ULTIMATE LOSS

That evening, Kit lay in bed in her room. She couldn't even call it her and Anya's room anymore. Anya was gone. Between that and the House Cup disaster, she just wanted to lie there alone until she slowly withered away into dust.

Someone knocked softly and opened the door: Elaine. She stepped in and approached the bed.

"I'll save you the trouble," Kit said without moving. "Yes, I totally made a big mess and we lost to the boys and I let you down. I get it. I'm probably even responsible for us losing Anya. I'll report to Lady C and beg her to take me off the roster so I don't ruin the rest of your life." Kit waited to hear agreement from Lamination Queen Super-Student Miss Perfect, but she heard only silence.

Then Elaine said softly, "Look, everyone has a bad course. Even when they're experienced. Even me. But you did it."

"I didn't do anything except argue with that impossible four-legged nightmare."

Again Elaine paused. Then: "Do you know what you did wrong?"

That was enough to give Kit the energy to sit up. "Yes, please, make me a list! Start with packing up and coming to this school and driving away the best friend I've ever made!" She was so mad at everything and everybody that she hoped Elaine would yell back. At least if they had a good argument, they would both get it out of their systems.

Elaine surprised her. She perched on the edge of Kit's bed and said, "You didn't listen to your horse. He was trying to tell you that he couldn't handle it, but you weren't hearing him. You just cared about what *you* wanted to do."

Even through all of the anguish and confusion in her head, Kit heard those words, and they rang true. She had let TK down.

Juniper Cottage was full of noisy celebration. The house common room had been decorated by Alex and Wyatt, whose idea of "decorations" were long strips of brightly colored paper thrown everywhere. *Everywhere.*

Will stood in the doorway and admired the mess. It was like an old-fashioned ticker-tape parade he'd seen in black-and-white movies. It looked like snow, there would be so much of it thrown everywhere. Very festive, but whenever Will saw one of those scenes, he always wondered who had to clean it up afterward. *He* certainly wasn't going to clean up *this* mess, that was for sure, though it had been a blast jumping around with the other boys throwing fistfuls of paper around, hooting and hollering in victory while music blared from Leo's iPod.

Leo, Alex, Wyatt, and their friends were still partying, but Will was ready to turn in. It had been a hard day. As he passed the house's little kitchen on the way to the stairs, he saw Nav, alone, making himself a cup of tea. He hurried past, not wanting to interact. He was still miffed at Nav, even though revenge had been nicely achieved that afternoon. Still, the whole thing made him feel itchy.

When he stepped into his dorm room, he found Josh lying on the bed, earbuds on, listening to music on his phone. "Oi!" Will snapped. "What are you doing in my room? You did not beat me! You could not beat the Master!" He held the door open. "Get out."

"*Au contraire*, my friend," said a very happy Josh. "See, I only had to beat Nav, which I did." He pointed to a bunch of boxes on the floor. "Your stuff's all ready. Enjoy rooming with Leo. I would invest in some earplugs, though. That dude snores like a chainsaw."

Will wanted to argue, but Josh, blast him, was right. With a growl, Will picked up a box of his stuff and headed for the room with the human chainsaw.

Late that night, after everybody had retired to their rooms, Kit donned her coat, tugged on her boots, and sneaked out to the stables. TK somehow knew she was coming, because, as she approached, he stuck his head out of his stall and turned in her direction, ears alert.

Kit threw her arms around his neck. "I am so sorry," she told him. "I promise I will never do that ever again." She stood back, petting his neck.

TK snorted and nodded.

"Does that mean you forgive me?" Kit asked. "Because it would be terrible if we were fighting. I don't know what I would do without you."

She heard footsteps and turned to find two men approaching TK's stall. One of them was holding a lead rope.

Something wasn't right.

"Can I help you?" Kit asked them.

At the same time, in Lady Covington's office, Rudy was trying to reason with the furious headmistress. "Will's a kid who needs to ride," he told her, trying to make his voice respectful but convincing. "He should be given credit for all the hours he spent helping Kit. Look, if I'm the stable master, I've got to have some say in all this."

"I am talking about Katherine!" Lady Covington snapped. "How could you let her put herself in danger?"

Rudy didn't even try to hold back his feelings on this one. "Oh, that's rich," he muttered, loud enough for her to hear. "It was your schedule that pushed her so hard."

"She could have been hurt!"

"I know! But you've been telling her for weeks that her inability to ride is some sort of moral failure! And threatening to take TK away? What do you think that was teaching her?"

"This will not happen again. You are on probation."

Rudy stood up. "I was right there. She's my daughter." He jabbed at finger at Lady Covington, not caring if she fired him on the spot. "Don't forget that."

Standing tall, Lady Covington did not fire him, but her words did chill his soul. "You'd better go and see her. She'll need you more than ever now."

That was a red flag warning if Rudy ever heard one. "Why?" he demanded. Good grief, what had Lady Covington done to his daughter now?

Knowing he'd get no straight answer from her, he left her office without saying good-bye and, on instinct, went straight to the stables. He was just in time to see a truck pulling a horse trailer drive out of the courtyard. Kit was running after it, screaming, *"Stop! Stop!"* She was crying. "TK!" She started a slow fall to the ground, but Rudy reached her fast enough to grab hold of her as she whimpered, "No . . ."

For the first time since his wife had died, Rudy Bridges had no idea what to do, so he just held Kit tight in his arms as she wept.

This book is based on the television series *Ride*.

Copyright © 2018 by Breakthrough Entertainment

First edition 2018

Library of Congress Catalog Card Number pending
ISBN 978-0-7636-9854-6 (hardcover)
ISBN 978-0-7636-9855-3 (paperback)

18 19 20 21 22 23 BVG 10 9 8 7 6 5 4 3 2 1

Printed in Berryville, VA, U.S.A.

This book was typeset in Caslon 450.

Candlewick Entertainment
an imprint of
Candlewick Press
99 Dover Street
Somerville, Massachusetts 02144

visit us at www.candlewick.com